Emily Sarah Holt

The King's Daughters

How Two Girls Kept the Faith

Emily Sarah Holt

The King's Daughters
How Two Girls Kept the Faith

ISBN/EAN: 9783743403550

Manufactured in Europe, USA, Canada, Australia, Japa

Cover: Foto ©Andreas Hilbeck / pixelio.de

Manufactured and distributed by brebook publishing software (www.brebook.com)

Emily Sarah Holt

The King's Daughters

The

King's Daughters

How Two Girls kept the Faith

BY

EMILY SARAH HOLT

AUTHOR OF "ONE SNOWY NIGHT," "MISTRESS MARGERY,"
"SISTER ROSE" ETC

NEW EDITION

LONDON:
PICKERING & INGLIS,
14, PATERNOSTER ROW, E.C.4,
AND
229, BOTHWELL STREET, GLASGOW,
or through any bookseller.

CONTENTS.

Contents.

THE KING'S DAUGHTERS.

CHAPTER I.

CHOOSING A NEW GOWN.

IVE you good den, Master Clere!" said a rosy-faced countrywoman with a basket on her arm, as she came into one of the largest clothier's shops in Colchester. It was an odd way of saying "Good Evening," but this was the way in which they said it in 1556. The rosy-faced woman set down her basket on the counter, and looked round the shop in the leisurely way of somebody who was in no particular hurry. They did not dash and rush and scurry through their lives in those days, as we do in these. She was looking to see if any acquaintance of hers was there. As she found nobody she went to business. "Could you let a body see a piece of kersey, think you? I'd fain have a brown or a good dark murrey[1] 'd serve me—somewhat that should not show dirt, and may be trusted to wear

---

[1] Mulberry-colour, much like that we call plum-colour or prune.

well.—Good den, Mistress Clere!—Have you e'er a piece o' kersey like that?"

Master Nicholas Clere, who stood behind the counter, did not move a finger. He was a tall, big man, and he rested both hands on his counter, and looked his customer in the face. He was not a man whom people liked much, for he was rather queer-tempered, and as Mistress Clere was wont to remark, "a bit easier put out than in." A man of few words, but those were often pungent, was Nicholas Clere.

"What price?" said he.

"Well! you mustn't ask me five shillings a yard," said the rosy-faced woman, with a little laugh. That was the price of the very best and finest kersey.

"Shouldn't think o' doing," answered the clothier.

"Come, you know the sort as 'ill serve me. Shilling a yard at best. If you've any at eightpence—"

"Haven't."

"Well, then I reckon I must go a bit higher."

"We've as good a kersey at elevenpence," broke in Mrs. Clere, "as you'd wish to see, Alice Mount, of a summer day. A good brown, belike, and not one as 'll fade—and a fine thread—for the price, you know. You don't look for kersey at elevenpence to be even with that at half-a-crown, now, do you? but you'll never repent buying this, I promise you."

Mrs. Clere was not by any means a woman of few words. While she was talking her husband had taken down the kersey, and opened it out upon the counter.

"There!" said he gruffly: "take it or leave it."

There were two other women in the shop, to whom Mrs. Clere was showing some coarse black stockings: they looked like mother and daughter. While Alice Mount was looking at the kersey, the younger of these two said to the other—

"Isn't that Alice Mount of Bentley?—she that was had to London last August by the Sheriffs for heresy, with a main lot more?"

"Ay, 'tis she," answered the mother in an undertone.

" Twenty-three of them, weren't there?"

'Thereabouts. They stood to it awhile, if you mind, and then they made some fashion of submission, and got let off."

" So they did, but I mind Master Maynard said it was but a sorry sort. He wouldn't have taken it, quoth he."

The other woman laughed slightly. " Truly, I believe that, if he had a chance to lay hold on 'em else. He loves bringing folk to book, and prison too."

" There's Margaret Thurston coming across," said the younger woman, after a moment's pause. " I rather guess she means to turn in here."

When people say " I guess " now, we set them down at once as Americans; but in 1556 everybody in England said it. Our American cousins have kept many an old word and expression which we have lost.[1]

In another minute a woman came in who was a strong contrast to Alice Mount. Instead of being small, round, and rosy, she was tall and spare, and very pale, as if she might have been ill not long before. She too carried a basket, but though it was only about half as large as Alice's, it seemed to try her strength much more.

"Good den, neighbour!" said Alice, with a pleasant smile.

"Good den, Alice. I looked not to find you here. What come you after?"

---

[1] They say, " I want to *have you go*," when we should say, " I want *you to go*." Queen Elizabeth would have used the former expression.

"A piece of kersey for my bettermost gown this summer. What seek you?"

"Well, I want some linsey for mine. Go you on, and when you've made an end I'll ask good Master Clere to show me some, without Mistress Clere's at liberty sooner."

Alice Mount was soon satisfied. She bought ten yards of the brown kersey, with some black buckram to line it, and then, as those will who have time to spare, and not much to occupy their thoughts, she turned her attention to helping Margaret Thurston to choose her gown. But it was soon seen that Margaret was not an easy woman to satisfy. She would have striped linsey; no, she wouldn't, she would have a self colour; no, she wouldn't, she would have a little pattern; lastly, she did not know which to have! What did Master Clere think? or what would Alice recommend her?

Master Clere calmly declined to think anything about it.

"Take it or leave it," said he. "You'll have to do one or t'other. Might as well do it first as last."

Margaret turned from one piece to another with a hopelessly perplexed face. There were three lying before her; a plain brown, a very dark green with a pretty little pattern, and a delicate grey, striped with a darker shade of the same colour.

"Brown's usefullest, maybe," said she in an uncertain tone. "Green's none so bad, though. And that grey's proper pretty—it is a gentlewoman's gown. I'd like that grey."

The grey was undoubtedly ladylike, but it was only fit for a lady, not for a working man's wife who had cooking and cleaning to do. A week of such work would ruin it past repair.

"You have the brown neighbour," said Alice. It's

not the prettiest, maybe, but it 'll look the best when it's been used a while. That grey 'll never stand nought; and the green, though it's better, 'll not wear even to the brown. You have the brown now."

Still Maragret was undecided. She appealed to Mrs. Clere.

"Why, look you," responded that talkative lady, "if you have yonder green gown, you can don it of an even when your master comes home from work, and he'll be main pleased to see you a-sitting in the cottage door with your bit o' needlework, in a pretty green gown."

"Aye, so he will!" said Margaret, suddenly making up as much mind as she had. "I thank you Mistress Clere. I'll have the green, Master Clere, an' it please you."

Now, Alice Mount had offered a reason for choosing the brown dress, and Mrs. Clere had only drawn a picture; but Margaret was the sort of woman to be influenced by a picture much more than by a solid reason. So the green linsey was cut off and rolled up—not in paper: that was much too precious to be wasted on parcels of common things. It was only tied with string, and each woman taking her own package, the two friends were about to leave the shop, when it occurred to Mrs. Mount to ask a question.

"So you've got Bessy Foulkes at last, Mistress Clere?"

"Aye, we have, Alice," was the answer. "And you might have said, ' at long last,' trow. Never saw a maid so hard to come by. I could have got twenty as good maids as she to hire themselves, while Bess was thinking on it."

"She should be worth somewhat, now you have her, if she took such work to come by," observed Margaret Thurston.

"Oh, well, she'll do middling. She's a stirring maid over her work: but she's mortal quiet, she is. Not a word can you get out of her without 'tis needed. And for a young maid of nineteen, you know, that's strange fashions."

"Humph!" said Master Nicholas, rolling up some woollen handkerchiefs. "The world 'd do with another or twain of that fashion."

"Now, Nicholas, you can't say you get too much talk!" exclaimed his wife turning round. "Why Amy and me, we're as quiet as a couple of mice from morning till night. Aren't we now?"

"Can't I?" said Nicholas, depositing the handkerchiefs on a shelf.

"Well, any way, you've got no call to it. Nobody can say I talk too much, that I know: nor yet Amy."

"You know, do you?" said her husband coolly. "Well, then, I need not to say it."

"Now, neighbours, isn't that too bad?" demanded Mrs. Clere, as Nicholas moved away to attend to another customer. "I never was a rattle, not I. But 'tis right like men: they take in their heads that all women be talkers, and be as still as you will, they shall write you down a chatterbox. Well, now, can't I tempt you with nought more? Stockings, or kerchiefs, or a knitted cap? Well, then, good den. I don't so well like the look of them clouds yonder; we shall have rain afore night, take my word for it. Farewell!"

CHAPTER II

HE clothier's shop which we entered in the last chapter was in Balcon or Balkerne Lane, not far from its northern end. The house was built, as most houses then were, with the upper storey projecting beyond the lower, and with a good deal of window in proportion to the wall. The panes of glass were very small, set in lead, and of a greenish hue; and the top of the house presented two rather steeply sloped gables. Houses in that day were more picturesque than they have been for the last two hundred years, though they have shown a tendency in recent times to turn again in that direction. Over Master Clere's door—and over every door in the street—hung a signboard, on which some sign was painted, each different from the rest, for signs then served the purpose of numbers, so that two alike in the same street would have caused confusion. As far as eye could see ran the gaily-painted boards —Blue Lion, varied by red, black, white, and golden lions; White Hart, King's Head, Golden Hand, Vine, Wheelbarrow, Star, Cardinal's Hat, Crosskeys, Rose, Magpie, Saracen's Head, and Katherine Wheel. Master Nicholas Clere hung out a magpie: why, he best knew, and never told. His neighbours sarcastically said that it was because a magpie lived there, meaning Mistress

Clere, who was considered a chatterbox by everybody except herself.

Our two friends, Margaret Thurston and Alice Mount, left the shop together, with their baskets on their arms, and turning down a narrow lane to the left, came out into High Street, down which they went, then along Wye Street, and out at Bothal's Gate. They did not live in Colchester, but at Much Bentley, about eight miles from the town, in a south-easterly direction.

"I marvel," said Margaret, as the two pursued their way across the heath, "how Bessy Foulkes shall make way with them twain."

"Do you so?" answered Alice. "Truly, I marvel more how she shall make way with the third."

"What, Mistress Amy?"

Alice nodded.

"But why? There's no harm in her, trow?"

"She means no harm," said Alice. "But there's many an one, Meg, as doesn't mean a bit of harm, and does a deal for all that. I'm feared for Bessy."

"But I can't see what you're feared for."

"These be times for fear," said Alice Mount. "Neighbour, have you forgot last August?"

"Eh! no, trust me!" cried Margaret. "Didn't I quake for fear, when my master came in, and told me you were taken afore the justices! "Truly, I reckoned he and I should come the next. I thank the good Lord that stayed their hands!"

"'Tis well we be on the Heath," said Alice, glancing round, as if to see whether they could be overheard. "If we spake thus in the streets of Colchester, neighbour, it should cost us dear."

"Well, I do hate to be so careful!"

"Folks cannot have alway what they would," said Alice. "But you know, neighbour, Bessy Foulkes is one of us."

"Well, what then ? So's Master Clere."

Alice made no answer.

"What mean you, Alice Mount? Master Clere's a Gospeller, and has been this eight years or more."

"I did not gainsay it, Meg."

"Nay, you might not gainsay it, but you looked as if you would if you opened your mouth."

"Well, neighbour, my brother at Stoke Nayland sells a horse by nows and thens: and the last time I was yonder, a gentleman came to buy one. There was a right pretty black one, and a bay not quite so well-looking. Says the gentleman to Gregory, 'I'd fainer have the black, so far as looks go; but which is the better horse ?' Quoth Gregory, 'Well, Master, that hangs on what you mean to do with him. If you look for him to make a pretty picture in your park, and now and then to carry you four or five mile, why, he'll do it as well as e'er a one; but if you want him for good, stiff work, you'd best have the bay. The black's got no stay in him,' saith he. So, Meg, that's what I think of Master Clere—he's got no stay in him. I doubt he's but one of your fair-weathered folks, that'll side with Truth when she steps bravely forth in her satin gown and her velvet slippers; but when she comes in a threadbare gown and old clouted shoes, then she's not for their company. There's a many of that sort."

"And you think Master Clere's one ? " said Margaret, in a tone which sounded as if she did not think so.

"I'm feared he is. I'd not say it if there wasn't need. But if you see Bess afore I do—and you are more like, for you go into town oftener—do drop a word to her to be prudent."

"Tell Elizabeth Foulkes to be prudent ! " exclaimed Margaret, laughing. "Nay, that were carrying coals o Newcastle ! "

"Well, and the day may come for that, if the pits there be used up. Meg, have you ne'er noted that folks oftener come to trouble for want of their chief virtue than from overdoing it?"

"Nay, Alice, nor I don't think it, neither."

"Well, let be!" said Alice, shifting the basket to her other arm. "Them that lives 'll see it."

"But what mean you touching Mistress Amy? You said you were feared she'd make trouble for Bess."

"Ay, I am: but that's another matter. We've fault-found enough for one even. Who be them two afore us?"

"What, those bits of children? Why, they're two of Jack Johnson's, of Thorpe."

"They look as if they'd got too much to carry," said Alice, as they came up to the children. They were now about half way to Bentley.

The younger, a boy of about six, held one ear of a large jar full of meal, and the other was carried by his sister, whose apparent age was eight. They were plodding slowly along, as if afraid of spilling their meal, for the jar was pretty full.

"Well, Cis, thou hast there a load!" was Margaret's greeting.

The little girl turned her head to see who spoke, but she only said gravely, "Ay." A very grave, demure little maiden she seemed to be.

"Whither go you?" asked Alice Mount.

"We're going home," said the small boy.

"What, a matter of five miles, with that jar? Why, you'll drop in the road! Couldn't nobody have fetched it but you?"

"There wasn't nobody," said the little boy; and his sister looked up to say, in her grave way,—

'You know Mother's gone to Heaven."

" And who looks after you ? "

"Will looks after Baby," answered Cissy demurely
'and I look after Will."

"And who looks after thee?" asked Alice much
amused.

"I'm older than I look," replied Cissy, drawing
herself up ; but she was not big enough to go far.

"I'm nine—going in ten. I can make porridge, and
clean the room and wash Baby. And Will's learning
to wash himself, and then he'll be off my hands."

It was irresistibly funny to hear this small mite talk
like a woman, for she was very small of her age; and
Alice and Margaret could not help laughing.

"Well, but thou knowest thou canst not do a many
things that must be done. Who takes care of you all ?
I dare be bound thou does thy best: but somebody
there must be older than thee. Who is it now ? "

" Have you e'er an aunt or a grandmother ? " added
Margaret.

Cissy looked up quietly into Alice's face.

"God takes care of us," she said. "Father helps
when his work's done; but when he's at work, God
has to do it all. There's nobody but God."

Alice and Margaret looked at each other in astonishment.

" Poor little souls ! " cried Margaret.

"Oh, but we aren't ! " said Cissy, rather more eagerly.
"God looks after us, you know. He's sure to do it
right, Father says so."

Alice Mount laid her hand softly on Cissy's head.

" Ay, little maid, God will do it right," she said.
" But maybe He'd let me help too, by nows and thens.
Thou knowest the Black Bear at Much Bentley—corner
of lane going down to Thorpe ? "

Yes, Cissy knew the Black Bear, as her face showed.

"Well, when thou gets to the Black Bear, count three doors down the lane, and thou'lt see a sign with a bell. That's where I live. Thee rap at the door, and my daughter shall go along with you to Thorpe, and help to carry the meal too. Maybe we can find you a sup of broth or milk while you rest you a bit."

"Oh, thank you!" said Cissy in her grown-up way. "That will be good. We'll come."

CHAPTER III.

ROSE.

"POOR little souls!" repeated Margaret Thurston, when the children were out of hearing.

Alice Mount looked back, and saw the small pair still toiling slowly on, the big jar between them. It would not have been a large jar for her to carry, but it was large and heavy too for such little things as these.

"However will they get home?" said she. "Nobody to look after them but 'God and Father'!"

The moment she had said it, her heart smote her. Was that not enough? If the Lord cared for these little ones, did it matter who was against them? How many unseen angels might there be on that road, watching over the safety of the children, and of that homely jar of meal for their sakes? It was not the first time that angels had attended to springs of water and cakes baken on the coals. No angel would dream of stopping to think whether such work degraded him. It is only men who stoop low enough for that. The highest work possible to men or angels is just doing the will of God: and God was the Father of these little ones.

"What is their Father?" asked Alice Mount.

"Johnson? Oh, he is a labouring man—a youngish man, only four-and-thirty: his mistress died a matter of six months back, and truly I know not how those bits of children have done since."

"They have had ' God and Father,' " said Alice

"Well, I've no doubt he's a good father," answered Margaret. "John Johnson is as good a man as ever stepped, I'll say that for him : and so was Helen a rare good woman. I knew her well when we were maids together. Those children have been well fetched up, take my word for it."

"It must have been a sad matter to lose such a wife," said Alice.

"Well, what think you ? " answered Margaret, dropping her voice. "Agnes Love told me—Jack Love's wife, that dwells on the Heath—you'll maybe know her?"

"Ay, I know her, though not well."

"I've known her ever since she was a yard long. Well, she told me, the even it happed came Jack Johnson to their house, and when she oped the door, she was fair feared of him, he looked so strange—his face all white, and such a glitter of his eyes—she marvelled what had taken him. And says he, ' Agnes, my Helen's gone.' ' Gone ? oh dear ! ' says she. ' Ay, she's gone, thank God ! ' says he. Well, Agnes thought this right strange talk, and says she, ' Jack Johnson, what can you mean ? Never was a better woman than your Helen, and you thanking God you've lost her ! ' ' Nay, Agnes, could you think that ? ' says he. ' I'm thanking God because now I shall never see her stand up on the waste by Lexden Road,' says he. ' She's safe from that anguish for evermore ! ' And you know what that meant."

Yes, Alice Mount knew what that meant—that allusion to the waste ground by Colchester town wall on the road to Lexden, where the citizens shot their rubbish, and buried their dead animals, or threw them

unburied, and burned their martyrs. It was another
way of saying what the Voice from Heaven had cried
to the Apostle—"Blessed are the dead that die in the
Lord from henceforth!"

"It's a marvel they haven't done somewhat to them
Loves afore now," said Margaret, after a minute's silence.

"I thought they had?" replied Alice. "Wasn't
John Love up afore the Sheriff once at any rate?"

"Oh, ay, they've had him twice o'er; don't you
mind they gat them away in the night the last time,
and all his goods was taken to the Queen's use? But
now, see, he's come back, and they let him alone.
They've done all they mean to do, I reckon."

"God grant it!" said Alice, with a sigh. "Meg, I
cannot forget last August. Twenty-two of us had up
afore the Bishop, and we only escaped by the very skin
of our teeth, as saith Job. Aye me! I sometimes
marvel if we did well or no, when we writ our names to
that submission."

"Truly, neighbour, so have I," replied Margaret
rather bluntly. "I would not have set mine thereto, I
warrant you."

Alice sighed heavily. "God knoweth we meant not
to deny His truth," said she; "and He looketh on the
heart."

After that they were silent till they came to Much
Bentley. Turning down the lane which led to Thorpe,
they came in sight of a girl of twenty years, sitting on
a low stool at the door of the third cottage in the lane,
weaving worsted lace on a pillow with bobbins. Over
the door hung a signboard bearing a bell painted blue.
The lace-maker was a small-built girl, not in any way
remarkable to look at, with smooth dark hair, nicely kept,
and a rosy face with no beauty about it, but with a
bright, kind-hearted expression which was better than

outside beauty. If a person accustomed to read faces had been there, he might perhaps have said that the small prominent chin, and the firm setting of the lips, suggested that Rose Allen occasionally had a will of her own. The moment that Rose saw who was coming, she left her stool with a bright smile which lighted up all her face, and carrying the stool in one hand, and her lace pillow in the other, disappeared within the house.

"She's quick at her work, yonder maid," said Margaret.

"Ay, she's a good lass, my Rose!" was her mother's answer. "You'll come in and sit a bit, neighbour?"

"Well, thank you, I don't mind if I do—at any rate till them children comes up," responded Margaret, with a little laugh. "Will you have me while then?"

"Ay, and as long after as you've a mind," said Alice heartily, leading the way into her cottage.

As Margaret had a mile yet to walk, for she lived midway between Much Bentley and Thorpe, she was glad of a rest. In the kitchen they found Rose, very busy with a skillet over the fire. There was no tea in those days, so there was no putting on of the kettle: and Rose was preparing for supper a dish of boiled cabbage, to which the only additions would be bread and cheese. In reply to her mother's questions, she said that her stepfather had been in, but finding his wife not yet come from market, he had said that he would step into the next neighbour's until she came, and Rose was to call him when supper was ready.

William Mount, the second husband of Alice, was twenty years older than his wife, their ages being sixty-one and forty-one. He was a tall, grey, grave-looking man,—a field labourer, like most of the dwellers in Much Bentley. This was but a small place, nestling at one corner of the large park of the Earl of Oxford,

the owner of all the property for some distance round.
Of course he was *the* great man in the esteem of the
Much Bentley people. During the reign of Edward
the Sixth, when Protestantism was in favour at Court,
Lord Oxford had been a Protestant like other people :
but, also like many other people, he was one of those of
whom it has been well said that

> " He's a slave who dare not be
> In the right with two or three."

Lord Oxford was a slave in this sense—a slave to
what other people said and thought about him—and
very sad slavery it is. I would rather sweep a crossing than feel that I did not dare to say what I believed
or disbelieved, what I liked or did not like, because
other people would think it strange. It is as bad as
being in Egyptian bondage. Yet there are a great
many people quite contented to be slaves of this kind,
who have not half so much excuse as Lord Oxford. If
he went against the priests, who then were masters of
everything, he was likely to lose his liberty and property,
if not his life; while we may say any thing we like
without need to be afraid. It is not always an advantage to have a great deal to lose. The poor labourers of
Much Bentley, who had next to no property at all, and
could only lose liberty and life, were far braver than
the Earl whom they thought such a grand man, and
who carried a golden wand before the Queen.

Supper was over at the Blue Bell, and Margaret
Thurston was thinking about going home, when a little
faint rap came on the door of the cottage. Rose opened
it, and saw a big jar standing on the door-sill, a little
boy sitting beside it, and an older girl leaning against
the wall.

" Please, we're come," said Cissy.

CHAPTER IV.

ON THE WAY TO THORPE.

LEASE, we're come," said Cissy. "We've been a good while getting here, but we—— Oh, it isn't you!"

"What isn't me?" said Rose, laughing—for people said *me* where it should have been *I*, then, as they do still. "I rather think it is me; don't you?"

"Yes, but you are not she that spake to us on the road," said Cissy. "Somebody told us to call here as we went down the lane, and her daughter should go home with us, and help us to carry the big jar. Perhaps you're the daughter?"

"Well, I guess I am," answered Rose. "Where's home?"

"It's at the further end of Thorpe."

"All right. Come in and rest you, and I'll fetch a sup of something to do you good, poor little white faces."

Rose took a hand of each and led them forward.

"Mother, here be two bits of Maypoles," said she, "for they be scarce fatter; and two handfuls of snow, for they be scarce rosier—that say you promised them that I should go home with them and bear their jar of meal."

"So I did, Rose. Bring them in, and let them warm themselves," answered Mrs. Mount. "Give them a sup of broth or what we have, to put a bit of life in them; and at after thou shalt bear them company to Thorpe. Poor little souls! they have no mother, and they say God looks after them only."

"Then I shall be in His company too," said Rose softly. Then, dropping her voice that the children might not hear, she added, " Mother, there's only that drop of broth you set aside for breakfast; and it's scarce enough for you and father both. Must I give them that?"

Alice Mount thought a moment. She had spoken before almost without thinking.

"Daughter," she said, " if their Father, which is also ours, had come with them visible to our eyes, we should bring forth our best for Him; and He will look for us to do it for the little ones whose angels see His Face. Aye, fetch the broth, Rose."

Perhaps Cissy had overheard a few words, for when the bowl of broth was put into her hands, she said, "Can you spare it? Didn't you want it for something else than us?"

"We can spare it, little maid," said Alice, with a smile.

"Sup it up," added Rose, laying her hand on the child's shoulder; "and much good may it do thee! Then, when you are both warmed and rested, I'll set forth with you."

Cissy did not allow that to be long. She drank her broth, admonished Will by a look to finish his—for he was disposed to loiter,—and after sitting still for a few minutes, rose and put down the bowl.

"We return you many thanks," she said in her prim little way, "and I think, if you please, we ought to go home. Father 'll be back by the time we get there; and I don't like to be away when he comes. Mother bade me not. She said he'd miss her worse if he didn't find me. You see, I've got to do for Mother now, both for Father and the children."

Alice Mount thought it very funny to hear this little mite talking about " the children," as if she were not a child at all.

"Well, tarry a minute till I tie on my hood," said Rose. " I'll be ready before you can say, ' This is the house that Jack built.' "

" What do you with the babe, little maid, when you go forth?" asked Alice.

"Baby?" said Cissy, looking up. "Oh, we leave her with Ursula Felstede, next door. She's quite safe till we come back."

Rose now came in from the inner room, where she had been putting on her hood and mantle. There were no bonnets then. What women called bonnets in those days were close thick hoods, made of silk, velvet, fur, or woollen stuff of some sort. Nor had they either shawls or jackets—only loose mantles, for out-door wear. Rose took up the jar of meal.

" Please, I can carry it on one side," said Cissy rather eagerly.

" Thou mayest carry thyself," said Rose. "That's plenty. I haven't walked five miles to-day. I'm a bit stronger than thou, too."

Little Will had not needed telling that he was no longer wanted to carry the jar; he was already off after wild flowers, as if the past five miles had been as many yards, though he had assured Cissy at least a dozen times as they came along that he did not know how he was ever to get home, and as they were entering Bentley had declared himself unable to take another step. Cissy shook her small head with the air of a prophetess.

"Will shouldn't say such things!" said she. "He said he couldn't walk a bit further—that I should have to carry him as well as the jar—and I don't know how I could, unless I'd poured the meal out and put him in, and he'd never have gone, I'm sure; and now, do but look at him after those buttercups!"

"He didn't mean to tell falsehoods," said Rose. "He was tired, I dare say. Lads will be lads, thou knowest."

"Oh dear, I don't know how I'm to bring up these children to be good people!" said Cissy, as gravely as if she had been their grandmother. "Ursula says children are great troubles, and I'm sure it's true. If there's any place where Will should be, that's just where he always isn't; and if there's one spot where he shouldn't be, that's the place where you commonly find him. Baby can't walk yet, so she's safe; but whatever I shall do when she can, I'm sure I don't know! I can't be in all the places at once where two of them shouldn't be."

Rose could not help laughing.

"Little maid," she said kindly, "thy small shoulders will never hold the world, nor even thy father's cottage. Hast thou forgot what thou saidst not an half-hour gone, that God takes care of you all?"

"Oh yes, He takes big care of us," was Cissy's answer. "He'll see that we have meat and clothes and so forth, and that Father gets work. But He'll hardly keep Will and Baby out of mischief, will He? Isn't that too little for Him?"

"The whole world is but a speck, little Cicely, compared with Him. If He will humble Himself to see thee and me at all, I reckon He is as like to keep Will out of mischief as to keep him alive. It is the very greatness of God that He can attend to all the little things in the world at once. They are all little things to Him. Hast thou not heard that the Lord Jesus said the very hairs of our heads be numbered?"

" Yea, Sir Thomas read that one eve at Ursula's."

Sir Thomas Tye was the Vicar of Much Bentley.

" Well," said Rose, " and isn't it of more importance to make Will a good lad than to know how many hairs he's got on his head? Wouldn't thy father think so?"

" For sure he would," said Cissy earnestly.

" And isn't God thy Father?"

Just as Rose asked that, a tall, dark figure turned out of a lane they were passing, and joined them. It was growing dusk, but Rose recognised the Vicar of whom they had just been speaking. Most priests were called " Sir " in those days.

" Christ bless you, my children!" said the Vicar.

Both Rose and Cissy made low courtesies, for great respect was then paid to a clergyman. They called them priests, for very few could read the Bible, which tells us that the only priest is our Lord Jesus Christ. A priest does not mean the same thing as a clergyman, though too many people thoughtlessly speak as if it did. A priest is a man who offers a sacrifice of some living thing to God. So, as Jesus Christ, who offered Himself, is our sacrifice, and there can never be any other, there cannot be any priests now. There are a great many texts which tell us this, but I will only mention one, which you can look out in your Bibles and learn by heart: the tenth verse of the tenth chapter of the Epistle to the Hebrews. It is easy to remember two tens.

Cissy was a little frightened when she saw that Sir Thomas walked on with them; but Rose marched on as if she did not care whether he came or not. For about a year after Queen Mary's accession, Sir Thomas had come pretty regularly to the prayer-meetings which were held sometimes at the Blue Bell, and sometimes at Ursula Felstede's at Thorpe, and also sometimes at John Love's on the Heath. He often read the Bible to them, and gave them little sermons, and seemed as kind and pleasant as possible. But when Queen Mary had been about a year on the throne, and it could be plainly seen which way things were going—that is, that she would try to bring back the Popish religion which her brother had cast off—Sir Thomas began to come less often. He found it too far to John Love's and to Thorpe; and whenever the meeting was at the Blue Bell, which was only a few hundred yards from the Vicarage,—well, it certainly was odd that Sir Thomas was always poorly on that night. Still, nobody liked to think that he was making believe; but Alice Mount said so openly, and Rose had heard her.

CHAPTER V

IN DIFFICULTIES.

CISSY JOHNSON was not old enough to understand all the reasons why her father distrusted the priest; but she knew well that "Father didn't like him," and like the dutiful little girl she was, she was resolved not to make a friend of any one whom her father disliked, for she knew that he might have good reasons which she could not understand. But Cissy had been taught to be civil to everybody, and respectful to her betters—lessons of which a little more would not hurt some folks in the present day. People make a great mistake who think that you cannot both be respectful to others and independent for yourself. The Bible teaches us to do both. Being in this state of mind, Cissy was decidedly pleased to see her father coming up from the other end of the lane.

"Oh, here's Father!" she said to Rose; and little Will ran on joyfully to meet him.

"Well, my lad!" was Johnson's greeting to his boy. "So thou and Cissy have got back? It's a right long way for such as thou."

Little Will suddenly remembered that he was exceedingly tired, and said so.

"Thou'd better go to bed," said his father, as they

came up with the girls. "Well, Cis, who hast thou
picked up?—I'm right thankful to you," he added,
looking at Rose, "for giving my little maid a helping
hand. It's a long way for such little ones, all the way
from the Heath, and a heavy load for little arms, and
I'm main thankful. Will you come in a bit and rest
you?" he said to Rose.

But Rose declined, for she knew her mother would
expect her to come back at once. She kissed Cissy,
and told her, whenever she had a load to carry either
way, to be sure she looked in at the Blue Bell, when
Rose would help her if she possibly could: and giving
the jar to Johnson, she bade him good-night, and turned
back up the lane. Sir Thomas had walked on, as Rose
supposed: at any rate, he was not to be seen. She
went nearly a mile without seeing any one, until Margaret Thurston's cottage came in sight. As Rose began
to go a little more slowly, she heard footsteps behind
her, and the next minute she was joined—to her surprise—by the priest.

"My daughter," he said, in a soft, kind voice, "I
think thou art Rose Allen?"

Rose dropped a courtesy, and said she was.

"I have been wishful to speak with some of thy
father's household," said Sir Thomas, in the same gentle
way: "so that I am fain to meet thee forth this even.
Tell me, my child, is there illness in the house or no?"

Rose breathed quickly: she guessed pretty well what
was coming.

"No, Father," she answered; "we are all in good
health, God be thanked for that same."

"Truly. I am glad to hear thee so speak, my daughter,
and in especial that thou rememberest to thank God.
But wherefore, then, being in good health, have ye not
come to give thanks to God in His own house, these

eight Sundays past? Ye have been regular aforetime, since ye were back from the Bishop's Court. Surely it is not true—I do hope and trust it is not true, that ye be slipping yet again into your past evil ways of ill opinions and presumptuous sin?"

The reason why the Mounts had not been to church was because the services were such as they could no longer join in. Queen Mary had brought back the Popish mass, and all the images which King Edward had done away with; so that to go to church was not to worship God but to worship idols. And so terrible was the persecution Mary had allowed to be set up, that the penalty for refusing to do this was to be burnt to death for what she called heresy.

It was a terrible position for a young girl in which Rose Allen stood that night. This man not only held her life in his hands, but also those of her mother and her step-father. If he chose to inform against them, the end of it might be death by fire. For one moment Rose was silent, during which she cried silently but most earnestly to God for wisdom and courage—wisdom to keep her from saying what might bring them into needless danger, and courage to stand true and firm to God and His truth.

"Might I be so bold as to pray you, Father," she said at last, "to ask at my mother the cause of such absence from mass? You wot I am but a young maid, and under direction of mine elders."

Sir Thomas Tye smiled to himself. He thought Rose a very cautious, prudent girl, who did not want to bring herself into trouble.

"So be it, my daughter," said he in the same gentle way. "Doubtless it was by direction of thine elders that thou wert absent aforetime, ere ye were had up to the Bishop."

He meant it as a question, by which he hoped to entangle poor Rose. She was wise enough not to answer, but to let it pass as if he were merely giving his own opinion, about which she did not wish to say anything.

"Crafty girl!" thought Sir Thomas. Then he said aloud,—"The festival of our Lady cometh on apace: ye will surely have some little present for our blessed Lady?"

The Virgin Mary was then called "Our Lady."

"We be but poor folks," said Rose.

"Truly, I know ye be poor folks," was the priest's reply. "Yet even poor folks do oft contrive to pleasure their friends by some little present. And if ye might bring no more than an handful of daisies from the field, yet is our Lady so gracious that she will deign to accept even so small an offering. Ye need not be empty-handed."

"I trust we shall do our duty," said poor Rose, in great perplexity. "Father, I cry you mercy if I stay me here, for I would fain speak with the woman of this cot."

"So do, my daughter," was the soft reply, "and I will call here belike, for I do desire to speak with Thurston."

Poor Rose was at her wit's end. Her little manœuvre had not succeeded as she hoped. She wanted to be rid of the unwelcome company of the priest; and now it seemed as if, by calling on Margaret Thurston instead of going straight home, she would only get more of it. However, she must do it now. She had nothing particular to say to Margaret, whom she had already seen that day, though her mother had said after Margaret was gone, that she wished she had told her something, and Rose meant to use this remark as furnishing an excuse.

She tapped, lifted the latch, and went in, the priest following.

John Thurston sat by the fire cutting clothes-pegs; Margaret was ironing clothes. Thurston rose when he saw the priest, and both received him reverently.

Feeling that her best chance of escaping the priest was to proceed immediately, Rose drew Margaret aside, and told her what her mother had said; but Margaret, who was rather fond of talking, had something to say too, and the precious minutes slid by. Meanwhile the priest and Thurston went on with their conversation: and at last Rose, saying she really could not stay any longer, bade them good-bye, and went out. But just as Margaret was opening the door to let her out, Sir Thomas said a few words in reply to Thurston, which Rose could not but overhear.

"Oh, Master Clere is a worthy man enough. If he hath gone somewhat astray in times past, that shall now be amended. Mistress Clere, too, is an honest woman that wist how to do her duty. All shall be well there. I trust, John Thurston, that thou shalt show thyself as wise and well ruled as he."

Rose heard no more. She passed out into the night, and ran nearly all the way home.

"Why, Rose, how breathless art thou, maid!" said the other when she came in.

"Well I may, Mother!" cried Rose. "There is evil ahead for us, and that not a little. Father Tye overtook me as I came back, and would know of me why we had not been to mass these eight Sundays; and I staved him off, and prayed him to ask of you. And, Mother, he saith Master Clere the draper, though he have gone somewhat astray, is now returned to his duty, and you wot what that meaneth. And I am 'feared for us, and Bessy too.

"The good Lord have mercy on us!" said Alice Mount.

"Amen!" responded William Mount gravely. "But it had best be such mercy as He will, Alice, not such as we would. On one matter I am resolved—I will sign no more submissions. I fear we have done it once too often."

"O Father, I'm so fain to hear you say it!" cried Rose.

"Art thou so, daughter?" he answered a little sadly. "Have a care thy quick tongue bring thee not into more trouble than need be. Child, to refuse that submission may mean a fiery death. And we may not—we must not—shrink from facing death for Him who passed through death for us. Lord, grant us Thy grace to stand true!"

And William Mount stood up with uncovered head, and looked up, as we all do instinctively when we speak to Him who dwelleth in the heavens.

"Who hath abolished death!" was the soft response of Alice.

CHAPTER VI.

ROSE ASKS A FAVOUR.

YOU'LL not find no better, search all Colchester through!" said Mrs. Clere, to a fat woman who did not look particularly amiable, holding up some worsted florence, drab with a red stripe.

"Well, I'm not so sure," replied the cross-looking customer. "Tomkins, now, in Wye Street, they showed me some Kendal frieze thicker nor that, and a halfpenny less by the yard."

"Tomkins!" said Mrs. Clere, in a tone not at all flattering to the despised Tomkins. "Why, if that man knows a Kendal frieze from a piece of black satin, it's all you can look for. Never bred up to the business, *he* wasn't. And his wife's a poor good-for-nought that wouldn't know which end of the broom to sweep with, and his daughters idle, gossiping hussies that'll drive their husbands wild one o' these days. Don't talk to me about Tomkins!"

And Mrs. Clere turned over the piece of florence as roughly as if it had been Tomkins instead of itself.

"It was right good frieze," said the customer doubtfully.

"Then you'd better go and buy it," snapped Mrs. Clere, whom something seemed to have put out that morning, for she was generally better-tempered than that.

"Well, but I'm not so sure," repeated the customer. "It's a good step to Wye Street, and I've lost a bit o' time already. If you'll take tenpence the ell, you may cut me off twelve."

"Tenpence the fiddlesticks!" said Mrs. Clere, pushing the piece of worsted to one side. "I'll not take a farthing under the shilling, if you ask me while next week. You can just go to Tomkins, and if you don't find you've got to darn his worthless frieze afore you've done making it up, why, my name isn't Bridget Clere, that's all. Now, Rose Allen, what's wanting?"

"An't please you, Mistress Clere, black serge for a girdle."

"Suit yourself," answered Mistress Clere, giving three pieces of serge, which were lying on the counter, a push towards Rose. "Well, Audrey Wastborowe, what are you standing there for? Ben't you a-going to that Tomkins?"

"Well, nay, I don't think I be, if you'll let me have that stuff at elevenpence the ell. Come now, do'ee, Mistress Clere!"

"I'm not to be coaxed, I tell you. Shilling an ell, and not a bit under."

"Well! then I guess I shall be forced to pay it. But you'll give me good measure?"

"I'll give you as many ells as you give me shillings, and neither more nor less. Twelve? Very good."

Mrs. Clere measured off the florence, tied it up, received the twelve shillings, which Audrey drew from her pocket as slowly as possible, perhaps fancying that Mrs. Clere might relent, and threw it into the till as if the coins were severely to blame for something. Audrey took up her purchase, and went out.

"Whatever's come to Mistress Clere?" asked a young woman who stood next to Rose, waiting to be served. "She and Audrey Wastborowe's changed tempers this morrow."

"Something's vexed her," said Rose. "I'm sorry, for I want to ask her a favour, when I've done my business."

"She's not in a mood for favour-granting," said the young woman. "That's plain. You'd better let be while she's come round."

"Nay, I can't let be," whispered Rose in answer.

"Now or never, is it? Well, I wish you well through it."

Mistress Clere, who had been serving another customer with an ounce of thread—there were no reels of thread in those days; it was only sold in skeins or large hanks—now came to Rose and the other girl.

"Good morrow, Gillian Mildmay! What's wanting?"

"Good morrow, Mistress Clere! My mother bade me ask if you had a fine marble cloth, about five shillings the ell, for a bettermost gown for her."

Mrs. Clere spoke a little less crossly, but with a weary air.

"Marbled cloth's not so much worn as it was," she said; "but I have a fair piece that may serve your turn. It's more nor that, though. I couldn't let it go under five and eightpence."

"Mother'll want it better cheap than that," said Gillian. "I think that'll not serve her, Mistress Clere. But I want a pair of tawny sleeves, an't like you, wrought with needlework."

Sleeves, at this time, were not a part of the dress, but were buttoned in as the wearer chose to have them. Gillian found these to suit her, paid for them, and went away. Mrs. Clere turned to Rose.

"Now, then, do be hasteful, Rose Allen; I'm that weary!"

"You seem so in truth, Mistress Clere. I'm feared you've been overwrought," said Rose, in a sympathising tone.

"Overwrought? Ay, body and soul too," answered Mrs. Clere, softening a little in response to Rose's tone. "Well! folks know their own troubles best, I reckon, and it's no good harrying other folks with them. What priced serge would you have?"

"About eighteenpence, have you some?"

"One and eightpence; and one and fourpence. The one-and-fourpenny's right good, you'll find."

"Thank you, I'll take the one-and-fourpenny: it'll be quite good enough for me. Well, I was going to ask you a favour, Mistress Clere; but seeing you look so o'erwrought, I have no mind to it."

"Oh, it's all in the day's work. What would you?" asked Mrs. Clere, rather more graciously.

"Well, I scarce like to tell you; but I *was* meaning to ask you the kindness, if you'd give leave for Bessy Foulkes to pass next saint's day afternoon with us. If you could spare her, at least."

"I can spare Bessy Foulkes uncommon well!" said Mrs. Clere irascibly.

"Why, Mistress Clere! Has Bessy——" Rose began in an astonished tone. Mrs. Clere's servant, Elizabeth Foulkes, was her dearest friend.

"You'd best give Mistress Elizabeth Foulkes the go-by, Rose Allen. She's a cantankerous, ill-beseen hussy, and no good company for you. She'll learn you to do as ill as herself, if you look not out."

"But what has Bessy done?"

"Gone into school-keeping," said Mrs. Clere sarcastically. "Expects her betters to go and learn their hornbook of her. Set herself up to tell all the world their duty, and knows it a sight better than they do

That's what Mistress Elizabeth's done and doing. Ungrateful hussy!"

"I couldn't have thought it!" said Rose, in a tone of great surprise, mixed with disappointment. "Bessy's always been so good a maid——"

"Good! don't I tell you she's better than every body else? Tell you what, Rose Allen, being good's all very well, but for a young maid to stick herself up to be better than her neighbours 'll never pay. I don't hold with such doings. If Bess'd be content to be the best cook, or the best cleaner, in Colchester, I'd never say nought to her; but she's not content; she'd fain be the best priest and the best school-master too. And that isn't her work, preaching isn't; dressing meat and scouring pans and making beds is what she's called to, and not lecturing folks at Market Cross."

"Has Bessy been preaching at the Market Cross?" asked Rose in genuine horror, for she took Mrs. Clere's statements literally.

"That's not while to-morrow," said Mrs. Clere in the same sarcastic tone. "She's giving the lecture at home first, to get perfect. I promise you I'm just harried out of my life, what with one thing and another!"

"Well, I'd like to speak with Bessy, if I might," said Rose in some perplexity. "We've always been friends, Bessy and me; and maybe she'd listen to me—or, any ways, to Mother. Could you kindly give leave for her to come, Mistress Clere?"

"You may have her, and keep her, for all the good she is to me," answered the clothier's wife, moving away. "Mind she doesn't give you the malady, Rose Allen: that's all I say! It's a fair infection going about, and the great doctors up to London 'll have to come down and look to it—see if they don't! Oh, my

lady can go if it like her—she's so grand now o' days
I'm very nigh afeared of her.   Good morrow ! ''

   And Rose went out with her parcel, lost in wonder as
to what could be the matter—first with Mistress Clere,
and then with her friend Elizabeth.

CHAPTER VII.

THE CLOUDS BEGIN TO GATHER.

ETHINKS that becomes me better
What sayest thou, Bess?"

Two girls were standing in an upper
room of Nicholas Clere's house, and the
younger asked this question of the elder.
The elder girl was tall, of stately carriage and graceful
mien, with a very beautiful face: but her whole aspect
showed that she thought nothing about herself, and
never troubled her head to think whether she was
pretty or ugly. The younger, who was about seventeen,
was not nearly so handsome; but she would have been
pleasant enough to look at if it had not been for a silly
simper and a look of intensely satisfied vanity, which
quite spoiled any prettiness that she might have had.
She had just fastened a pair of ear-rings into her ears,
and she was turning her head from one side to the
other before the mirror, as she asked her companion's
opinion of the ornaments.

There are some savages—in Polynesia, I think—who
decorate themselves by thrusting a wooden stick through
their lips. To our European taste they look hideous.
Honestly, I cannot see that they who make holes in
their lips in order to ornament themselves are any
worse at all than they who make holes in their ears for
the same purpose. The one is just as thorough bar-
barism as the other.

When Amy Clere thus appealed to her to express an opinion, Elizabeth Foulkes looked up from her sewing and gave it.

"No, Mistress Amy; I do scarce think it."

"Why, wouldst thou better love these yellow ones?"

"To speak truth, Mistress Amy, I think you look best without either."

"Dear heart, to hear the maid! Wouldst not thou fain have a pair, Bess?"

"Nay, Mistress Amy, that would I not."

"Wherefore?"

"Because, as methinks, such tawdry gewgaws be unworthy a Christian profession. If you desire my thought thereon, Mistress Amy, you have it now."

"Forsooth, and thou mightest have kept it, for all I want of it. 'Tawdry gewgaws,' indeed! I tell thee, Bess, these be three shillings the pair."

"They may be. I would not pay three half-pence for them."

"Bess, 'tis ten thousand pities thou art not a nun."

"I would rather be what I am, Mistress."

"I rather not be neither," said Amy flippantly. In those days, they always put two nots together when they meant to speak strongly. They did not see, as we do now, that the one contradicts the other.

"Well, Mistress Amy, you have no need," said Elizabeth quietly.

"And as to Christian profession—why, Bess, every lady in the land wears ear-rings, yea, up to the Queen's Grace herself. Prithee who art thou, to set thee up for better than all the ladies in England, talking of Christian profession as though thou wert a priest?"

"I am Mistress Clere's servant-maid; but I set not myself up to be better than any, so far as I know."

"Thee hold thy peace! Whether goeth this lace or the wide one best with my blue kirtle?"

"The narrower, I would say. Mistress Amy, shall you have need of me this next Wednesday afternoon?"

"Why? What's like to happen Wednesday afternoon?"

"Saint Chrysostom's like to happen, an't please you; and Mistress granted me free leave to visit a friend, if so be you lacked me not."

"What fashion of a friend, trow? A jolly one?" Elizabeth looked a little amused.

"Scarce after your fashion, Mistress Amy."

"What, as sad and sober as thyself?"

"Well-nigh."

"Then I'll not go with thee. I mean to spend St. Chrysostom with Mary Boswell and Lucy Cheyne, and their friends: and I promise thee we shall not have no sadness nor sedateness in the company."

"That's very like," answered Elizabeth.

"As merry as crickets, *we* shall be. Dost not long to come withal?"

"I were liefer to visit Rose, if it liked you."

"What a shame to call a sad maid by so fair a name! Oh, thou canst go for all me. Thy company's never so jolly I need shed tears to lose it."

And with this rather uncomplimentary remark, Amy left the room, with the blue ear-rings in her ears and the yellow ones in her hand. Elizabeth waited till her piece of work was finished. Then folding it up and putting it away in a drawer, she ran down to prepare supper,—a task wherein Amy did not offer to help her, though it was usual then for the mistress of the house and her daughters to assist in the cooking.

About two o'clock on the afternoon of the following Wednesday, a tap on the door of the Blue Bell called

Rose to open it, and she greeted her friend Elizabeth
with much pleasure. Rose had finished her share of
the household work (until supper), and she took her
lace pillow and sat down in the window. Elizabeth
drew from her pocket a couple of nightcaps, and both
girls set to work. Mrs. Mount was sewing also in the
chimney corner.

"And how be matters in Colchester, Bess, at this
present?"

"The clouds be gathering for rain, or I mistake,"
said Elizabeth gravely. "You know the thing I
mean?"

Alice Mount had put down her work, and she looked
grave too.

"Bess! you never mean we shall have last August's
doings o'er again?"

"That do I, Alice, and more. I was last night at
the King's Head, where you know they of our doctrine
be wont to meet, and Master Pulleyne was there, that
good man that was sometime chaplain to my Lady's
Grace of Suffolk: he mostly puts up at the King's
Head when he cometh to town. And quoth he, 'There
shall shortly be another search made for Gospel books,
—ay, and Gospellers belike: and they be not like
to 'scape so well as they did last year.' And John Love
saith—he was there, John Love of the Heath; you
know him?—well, he saith he heard Master Simnel the
bailiff to swear that the great Doctors of Colchester
should find it warm work ere long. There's an ill time
coming, friends. Take you heed."

"The good Lord be our aid, if so be!" said Alice.

"But what shall Master Clere do, Bessy?" asked
Rose. "He hath ever been a Gospeller."

"He hath borne the name of one, Rose. God
knoweth if he be true. I'm 'feared——"

Elizabeth stopped suddenly.

"That he'll not be staunch?" said Alice.

"He is my master, and I will say no more, Alice. But this may I say—there's many in Colchester shall bear faggots ere they burn. Ay, and all over England belike."

Those who recanted had to carry a faggot, as if owning themselves worthy to be burned.

"Thou'rt right there, Bess. The Lord deliver us!"

"Some thinketh we have been too bold of late. You see, John Love coming home again, and nothing done to him, made folks think the worst was over."

"Isn't it then?" said Rose.

"Master Benold says he misdoubts if 'tis well begun."

"Master Benold the chandler?"

"Of East Hill—ay. He was at the King's Head last night. So was old Mistress Silverside, and Mistress Ewring the miller's wife, and Johnson—they call him Alegar—down at Thorpe."

"Call him Alegar! what on earth for?" asked Rose indignantly.

Elizabeth laughed. "Well, they say he's so sour. He'll not dance, nor sing idle songs, nor play quoits and bowls, but loveth better to sit at home and read; so they call him Alegar."

Alegar is malt vinegar; the word vinegar was then used only of white wine vinegar.

"He's not a bit sour!" cried Rose. "I've seen him with his little lad and lass; and right good to them he was. It's a shame to call folks names that don't fit them!"

"Nay, I don't call him no names, but other folks do. Did you know his wife, that died six months gone?"

"No, but I've heard her well spoken of."

"Then you've heard truth. Those children lost

a deal when they lost her, and so did poor Johnson. Well, he'll never see her burn : that's one good thing !"

"Ay," said Alice, "and that's what he said himself when she died.   Well, God help us to stand firm ! Have you been asked any questions, Bess ? "

"Not yet," said Elizabeth quietly, "but I look for it every day.   Have you ? "

"Not I; but our Rose here foregathered with the priest one even of late, and he was set to know why we came not to church these eight weeks past.   She parried his darts right well; but I look to hear more thereabout."

CHAPTER VIII

NOT A BIT AFRAID.

LICE MOUNT had only just spoken when the latch was lifted by Margaret Thurston.

"Pray you, let me come in and get my breath!" said she; "I'm that frighted I can scarce stand."

"Come in, neighbour, and welcome," replied Alice; and Rose set a chair for Margaret. "What ails you? is there a mad bull about, or what?"

"Mad bull, indeed! A mad bull's no great shakes. Not to him, any way."

"Well, I'd as soon not meet one in our lane," said Alice; "but who's *him?*"

"*Him's* the priest, be sure! Met me up at top o' the lane, he did, and he must needs turn him round and walk by me. I well-nigh cracked my skull trying to think of some excuse to be rid of him; but no such luck for me! On he came till we reached hither, and then I could bear no more, and I said I had to see you. He said he went about to see you afore long, but he wouldn't come in to-day; so on he marched, and right thankful was I, be sure. Eh, the things he asked me! I've not been so hauled o'er the coals this year out."

"But what about, marry?"

"Gramercy! wherefore I came not to mass, and why Master didn't: and what I believed and didn't believe,

and wherefore I did this and didn't do that, till I
warrant you, afore he left off, I was that moithered I
couldn't have told what I did believe. I got so muggy
I only knew one thing under the sun, and that was that
I'd have given my best gown for to be rid of him."

"Well, you got free without your best gown, Margaret," said Rose.

"May be I have, but I feel as if I'd left all my wits
behind me in the lane, or mayhap in the priest's pocket.
Whatever would the man be at? We pay our dues to
the Church, and we're honest, peaceable folks: if it
serve us better to read our Bible at home rather than
go look at him hocus-pocussing in the church, can't he
let us be? Truly, if he'd give us something when we
came, there'd be some reason for finding fault; nobody
need beg me to go to church when there's sermon: but
what earthly good can it do any mortal man to stare at
a yellow cross on Father Tye's back? And what good
do you ever get beyond it?"

Sermons have always been a Protestant institution, in
this sense, that the more pure and Scriptural the Church
has been, the more sermons there have generally been,
while whenever the clergy have taken up with foolish
ceremonies and have departed from the Bible, they have
tried to do away with preaching. And of course, when
very few people could read their Bibles, there was more
need of preaching than there is now, when nearly
everybody can read. Very, very few poor people could
read a word in 1556. It was put down as something
remarkable, in the case of Cissy's father, that he could
" read a little." St. Paul says that it pleased God by
preaching to save them that believe (1 Cor. i. 21), but
he never says " by hearing music," or "by looking at
flowers, or candles, or embroidered crosses." Those
things can only amuse our eyes and ears; they will

never do our souls any good. How can they ? The only thing that will do good to our souls is to get to know God better: and flowers, candles, music, and embroidery, cannot teach us anything about God.

"What laugh you at, Rose ? " asked Elizabeth.

"Only Margaret's notion that it could do no man good to stare at the cross on Father Tye's back," said Rose, trying to recover her gravity.

"Well, the only animal made with a cross on his back is an ass," said Margaret; "and one would think a man should be better than an ass; but if his chief business be to make himself look like one, I don't see that he is so much better."

This amused Rose exceedingly. Elizabeth Foulkes, though the same age as Rose, was naturally of a graver turn of mind, and she only smiled.

"Well! if I haven't forgot all I was charged with, I'd better give my message," said Margaret; "but Father Tye 's well-nigh shook all my wits out of my head. Robin Purcas came by this morrow, and he lifted the latch, and gave me a word from Master Benold, that I was to carry on—for he's got a job of work at St. Osyth, and won't be back while Friday—saith he, on Friday even, Master Pulleyne and the Scots priest, that were chaplains to my Lady of Suffolk, shall be at the King's Head, and all of our doctrine that will come to hear shall be welcome. Will you go ? "

"Verily, that will I," replied Alice heartily.

"You see, if Father Tye should stir up the embers and get all alight again, maybe we shalln't have so many more sermons afterward; so we'd best get our good things while we can."

"Ay, there may be a famine of hearing the words of the Lord," said Alice gravely. "God avert the same, if His will is !"

'Johnson, he says he's right sure Master Simnel means to start of his inquirations. Alice, think you you could stand firm ? "

Alice Mount sighed and half shook her head. "I didn't stand over firm last August, Margaret," said she: "and only the Lord knows how I've since repented it. If He'll keep me true—but I'm feared of myself."

"Well, do you know I'm not a bit feared ? It's true, I wasn't tried in August, when you were: but if I had been, be sure I'd never have signed that submission that you did. I wouldn't, so ! "

"Maybe not, neighbour," answered Alice meekly. "I was weak."

"Now, Mother," said Rose, who could bear no longer, "you know you stood forth best of anybody there ! It was Father that won her to sign, Margaret ; she never would have done it if she'd been left to herself. I know she wouldn't."

"Then what didst thou sign for, Rose?" was the reply.

Rose went the colour of her name. Her mother came at once to her help, as Rose had just done to hers.

"Why, she signed because we did, like a dutiful maid as she is alway: and it was our faults, Margaret. May God forgive us ! "

"Well, but after all, it wasn't so very ill, was it?" asked Margaret, rather inconsistently with what she had said before: but people are not always consistent by any means. "Did you promise anything monstrous wrong ? I thought it was only to live as became good Christians and faithful subjects."

"Nay, Meg, it was more than that. We promised right solemnly to submit us to the Church in all matters, and specially in this, that we did believe the Sacrament to be Christ's body, according to His words."

"Why, so do we all believe," said Margaret, "*according to His words*. Have you forgot the tale Father Tye did once tell us at the King's Head, of my Lady Elizabeth the Queen's sister, that when she was asked what she did believe touching the Sacrament, she made this answer?—

> "'Christe was the Word that spake it,
> He took the bread, and brake it;
> And what that word did make it,
> That I believe, and take it.'"

"That was a bit crafty, methinks," said Rose. "I love not such shifts. I would rather speak out my mind plainly."

"Ay, but if you speak too plainly, you be like to find you in the wrong place," answered Margaret.

"That would not be the wrong place wherein truth set me," was Rose's earnest answer. "That were never the wrong place wherein God should be my company. And if the fire were too warm for my weakness to bear, the holy angels should maybe fan me with their wings till I came to the covert of His Tabernacle."

"Well, that's all proper pretty," said Margaret, "and like a book as ever the parson could talk: but I tell thee what, Rose Allen, thou'lt sing another tune if ever thou come to Smithfield. See if thou doesn't."

And Rose answered, "'The word that God putteth in my mouth, that will I speak.'"

CHAPTER IX.

DOROTHY DENNY, art thou never going to set that kettle on ?"

"Oh, deary me! a body never has a bit of peace ! "

"That's true enough of me, but it's right false of thee. Thou's nought but peace all day long, for thou never puts thyself out. I dare be bounden, if the Queen's Grace and all her noble company were to sup in this kitchen at five o' the clock, I should come in and find never a kettle nor a pan on at the three-quarter past. If thy uncle wasn't a sloth, and thine aunt a snail, I'm not hostess of the King's Head at Colchester. Thou'rt no more worth thy salt—nay, salt, forsooth! thou'rt not worth the water. Salt's one and fourpence the raser, and that's a deal too much to give for thee Now set me the kettle on, and then teem out that rubbish in the yard, and run to the nests to see if the hens have laid: don't be all day and night about it ! Run, Doll!—Eh deary me ! I might as well have said, Crawl. There she goes with the lead on her heels ! If these maids ben't enough to drive an honest woman crazy, my name's not Philippa Wade."

And Mistress Wade began to put things tidy in the kitchen with a promptitude and celerity which Dorothy Denny certainly did not seem likely to imitate. She

swept up the hearth, set a chair before the table, fresh
sanded the floor and arranged the forms in rows, before
Dorothy reappeared, carefully carrying something in her
apron.

"Why, thou doesn't mean to say thou'st done already?" inquired her mistress sarcastically. "Thou'st
been all across the yard while I've done no more than
sand the floor and side things for the gathering. What's
that in thine apron? one of the Queen's Majesty's
jewels?"

"It's an egg, Mistress."

"An egg! *an* egg?" demanded Mrs. Wade, with a
burst of hearty laughter; for she laughed, as she did
everything else, with all her might. "Is that all thou'st
got by thy journey? Marry, but I would have tarried
another day, and fetched two! Poor Father Pulleyne!
so he's but to have one egg to his supper? If them
hens have laid no more, I'm a Dutchwoman! See thou,
take this duster, and dust the table and forms, and I'll
go and search for eggs. If ever a mortal woman——"

Mistress Wade was in the yard before she got further,
and Dorothy was left to imagine the end of the sentence.
Before that leisurely young woman had finished dusting
the first form, the landlady reappeared with an apronful
of eggs.

"I marvel whither thou wentest for thy egg, Doll.
Here be eighteen thou leftest for me to gather. It's no
good to bid thee be 'shamed, for thou dost not know how.
I should in thy place, I'll warrant thee. Verily, I do
marvel whatever the world's a-coming to!"

Before Mrs. Wade had done more than empty her
apron carefully of the eggs, a soft rap came on the door;
and she called out,—

"Come within!"

"Please, I can't reach," said a little voice.

"Open the door, Doll," said Mrs. Wade; and in came three children—a girl of nine, a boy of six, and a baby in the arms of the former.

"Well, what are you after? Come for skim milk? I've none this even."

"No, please. Please, we're come to the preaching."

"*You're* come to the preaching? Why, you're only as big as mice, the lot of you. Whence come you?"

"Please, we've come from Thorpe."

. "You've come from Thorpe! you poor little bits of things! All that way!" cried Mrs. Wade, whose heart was as large as her tongue was ready. "Why, I do believe you're Cicely Johnson. You are so grown I didn't know you at first—and yet you're no bigger than a mouse, as I told you. Have you had any supper?"

"No, Mistress. Please, we don't have supper, only now and then. We shall do very well, indeed, if we may stay for the preaching."

"You'll sit down there, and eat some bread and milk, before you're an hour older. Poor little white-faced mortals as ever I did see! But you've never carried that child all the way from Thorpe?—Doll didst ever see such children?"

"They're proper peaked,[1] Mistress," said Dorothy.

"Oh no!" answered the truth-loving Cissy. "I only carried her from the Gate. Neighbour Ursula, she bare her all the way."

"Thou'rt an honest lass," said Mrs. Wade, patting Cissy on the head. "There, eat that."

And she put a large slice of bread into the hand of both Will and Cissy, setting a goodly bowl of milk on the table between them.

---

[1] Very thin and pinched-looking.

"That's good!" commented Will, attacking the milk-bowl immediately.

Cissy held him back, and looked up into Mrs. Wade's kindly and capacious face.

"But please we haven't got any money," she said anxiously.

"Marry come up![1] to think I'd take money from such bits of things as you! I want no money, child. The good Lord, He pays such bills as yours. And what set you coming to the preaching? Did your father bid you?"

"Father likes us to come," said Cissy, when her thanks had been properly expressed; "but he didn't bid us—not to-night. Mother, she said we must always come if we could. I'm feared Baby won't understand much: but Will and me, we'll try.'

"I should think not!" replied Mrs. Wade, laughing. "Why, if you and Will can understand aught that'll be as much as need be looked for. How much know you about it?"

"Please, we know about the Lord Jesus," said Cissy, putting her hands together, as if she were going to say her prayers. "We know that He died on the cross for us, so that we should not be punished for our sins, and He sends the Holy Ghost to make us good, and the Bible, which is God's Word, and we mustn't let anybody take it away from us."

"Well, if you know that much in your little hearts, you'll do," said the landlady. "There's many a poor heathen doesn't know half as much as that. Ay, child, you shall 'bide for the preaching if you want, but you're too soon yet. You've come afore the parson. Eat your bread and milk up, and 'bide where you are; that's a

---

[1] An exclamation of surprise, then often used.

snug little corner for you, where you'll be warm and safe. Is Father coming too, and Neighbour Ursula ? "

" Yes, they're both coming presently," said Cissy.

The next arrival was that of two gentlemen, the preacher and a friend. After this people began to drop in, at first by twos and threes, and as the time drew near, with more rapidity. The Mounts and Rose Allen came early; Elizabeth Foulkes was late, for she had hard work to get away at all. Last of anybody was Margaret Thurston and with her a tall, strong-looking man, who was John Thurston, her husband. John Johnson found out the corner where his children were, and made his way to them; but Rose Allen had been before him, and was seated next to Cissy, holding the little hand in hers. On the other side of little Will sat an old lady with grey hair, and a very sweet, kind face. She was Mrs. Silverside, the widow of a priest. By her was Mrs. Ewring the miller's wife, who was a little deaf, and wanted to get near the preacher.

When the room was full, Mr. Pulleyne, who was to preach that evening, rose and came forward to the table, and gave out the Forty-Second Psalm.

They had no hymn-books, as we have. There were just a few hymns, generally bound up at the end of the Prayer-Book, which had been written during the reign of good King Edward the Sixth ; but hardly any Englis' hymns existed at all then. They had one collection of metrical Psalms—that of Sternhold and Hopkins, of which we never sing any now except the Hundredth— that version known to every one, beginning—

" All people that on earth do dwell."

The Psalms they sang then sound strange to us now but we must remember they did not sound at all strai ge to those who sang them.　Here are two verses of the Forty-Second.

> " Like as the hart doth pant and bray,
>   The well-springs to obtain,
> So doth my soul desire alway
>   With Thee, Lord, to remain.
> My soul doth thirst, and would draw near
>   The living God of might;
> Oh, when shall I come and appear
>   In presence of His sight!

> " The tears all times are my repast,
>   Which from mine eyes do slide;
> Whilst wicked men cry out so fast,
>   ' Where now is God thy Guide ? '
> Alas ! what grief is it to think
>   The freedom once I had !
> Therefore my soul, as at pit's brink,
>   Most heavy is and sad."

CHAPTER X.

BROUGHT OUT, TO BE BROUGHT IN.

OUD and full rang the volume of voices in the kitchen of the King's Head at Colchester, that winter evening. They did not stand up in silence and let a choir do it for them, while they listened to it as they might to a German band, and with as little personal concern. When men's hearts are warm with patriotism, or overflowing with loyalty, they don't want somebody else to sing *Rule, Britannia,* or *God Save the Queen;* the very enjoyment lies in doing it themselves. Nobody would dream of paying another person to go to a party or to see a royal procession for him. Well, then, when we prefer to keep silent, and hear somebody sing God's praises instead of doing it ourselves, what can it mean except that our hearts are not warm with love and overflowing with thankfulness, as they ought to be? And cold hearts are not the stuff that makes martyrs.

There was plenty of martyr material in the King's Head kitchen that night—from old Agnes Silverside to little Cissy Johnson; from the learned priest, Mr. Pulleyne, to many poor men and women who did not know their letters. They were not afraid of what people would say, nor even of what people might do. And yet they knew well that it was possible, and even likely, that very terrible things might be done

to them. Their feeling was,—Well, let them be done,
if that be the best way I can glorify God. Let them be
done, if it be the way in which I can show that I love
Jesus Christ. Let them be done, if by suffering with
Him I can win a place nearer to Him, and send a thrill
of happiness to the Divine and human heart of the
Saviour who paid His heart's blood to ransom me.

So the hymn was not at all too long for them, though
it had fifteen verses; and the sermon was not too long,
though it lasted an hour and a half. When people have
to risk their lives to hear a sermon is not the time when
they cry out to have sermons cut shorter. They very
well knew that before another meeting took place at the
King's Head, some, and perhaps all of them, might be
summoned to give up liberty and life for the love of the
Lord Jesus.

Mr. Pulleyne took for his text a few words in the
23rd verse of the sixth chapter of Deuteronomy. " He
brought us out from thence, that He might bring us in."
He said to the people :—

"'He brought us out'—who brought us ? God, our
Maker; God, that loved the world. 'He brought us
out'—who be we ? Poor, vile, wicked sinners, worms
of the earth, things that He could have crushed easier
than I can crush a moth. From whence ? From Egypt,
the house of bondage; from sin, self, Satan—the only
three evil things there be : whereby I mean, necessarily
inwardly, utterly evil. Thence He brought us out.
Friends, we must come out of Egypt; out from bondage;
out of these three ill things, sin, and self, and Satan :
God will have us out. He will not suffer us to tarry in
that land. And if we slack [1] to come out, He will drive
us sharp thence. Let us come out quick, and willingly.

---

[1] Hesitate, feel reluctant.

There is nothing we need sorrow to leave behind; only the task-master, Satan; and the great monster, sin; and the slime of the river wherein he lieth hid, self. He will have at us with his ugly jaws, and bite our souls in twain, if we have not a care. Let us run fast from this land where we leave behind such evil things.

"But see, there is more than this. God had an intent in thus driving us forth. He did not bring us out, and leave us there. Nay, 'He brought us out that He might bring us in.' In where? Into the Holy Land, that floweth with milk and honey; the fair land where nothing shall enter that defileth; the safe land where in all the holy mountain nothing shall hurt nor destroy; His own land, where He hath His Throne and His Temple, and is King and Father of them that dwell therein. Look you, is not this a good land? Are you not ready to go and dwell therein? Do not the clusters of its grapes—the hearing of its glories—make your mouths water? See what you shall exchange: for a cruel taskmaster, a loving Father; for a dread monster, an holy City; for the base and ugly slime of the river, the fair paving of the golden streets, and the soft waving of the leaves of the tree of life, and the sweet melody of angel harps. Truly, I think this good barter. If a man were to exchange a dead rat for a new-struck royal,[1] men would say he had well traded, he had bettered himself, he was a successful merchant. Lo, here is worse than a dead rat, and better than all the royals in the King's mint. Will ye not come and trade?

"Now, friends, ye must not misconceive me, as though I did mean that men could buy Heaven by their own works. Nay, Heaven and salvation be free gifts—the glorious gifts of a glorious God, and worthy of the Giver. But

---

[1] Ten shillings; this was then the largest coin made.

when such gifts are set before you but for the asking, is it too much that ye should rise out of the mire and come?

"'He brought them out, that He might bring them in.' He left them not in the desert, to find their own way to the Holy Land. Marry, should they ever have come there? I trow not. Nay, no more than a babe of a month old, if ye set him down at Bothal's Gate, could find his way to the Moot Hall. But He dealt not with them thus. He left them not to find their own way. He brought them, He led them, He showed them where to plant their feet, first one step, then another, as mothers do to a child when he learneth first to walk. 'As a nurse cherisheth her children,' the Apostle saith he dealt with his converts: and the Lord useth yet tenderer image, for 'as a mother comforteth her babe,' saith He, 'will I comfort you.' Yea, He bids the Prophet Esaias to learn them, 'line upon line, precept upon precept, here a little and there a little'—look you, how careful is God of His nurse-children. 'Feed My Lambs,' saith He: and lambs may not nibble so hard as sheep. They take not so full a mouthful; they love the short grass, that is sweet and easily cropped. We be all lambs afore we be sheep. Sheep lack much shepherding, but lambs yet more. Both be silly things, apt to stray away, and the wolf catcheth them with little trouble. Now, if a dog be lost, he shall soon find his way back; but a lamb and a babe, if they be lost, they are utterly lost; they can never find the way. Look you, the Lord likeneth His people to lambs and babes, these silly things that be continually lost, and have no wit to find the way. So, brethren, *He* finds the way. He goeth after that which is lost, until He find it. First He finds the poor silly lamb, and then He leadeth it in the way wherein it shall go. He 'brings us in' to the fair green pastures and by the still waters—brings

us in to the safe haven where the little boats lie at rest
—brings us in to the King's banquet-hall where the
feast is spread, and the King Himself holdeth forth
hands of welcome. He stretched not forth the cold
sceptre; He giveth His own hand—that hand that was
pierced for our sins. What say I? Nay, 'He shall
gird Himself, and shall come forth and serve them '—
so great honour shall they attain which serve God, as to
have Him serve them.

" Now, brethren, is this not a fair lot that God ap-
pointeth for His people? A King to their guide, and a
throne to their bed, and angels to their serving-men—
verily these be folks of much distinction that be so
served! But, look you, there is one little point we may
not miss—'If we suffer, we shall reign.' There is the
desert to be passed. There is the Jordan to be forded.
There is the cross to bear for the Master that bare the
cross for us. Yea, we shall best bear our cross by looking well and oft on His cross. Ah! brethren, He standeth
close beside; He hath borne it all; He knoweth where
the nails run, and in what manner they hurt. Yet a little
patience, poor suffering soul! yet a little courage; yet
a little stumbling over the rough stones of the wilderness : and then the Golden City, and the royal banquet-
hall, and the King that brought us out despite all the
Egyptians, that brought us in despite all the dangers of
the desert,—the King, our Shield, and Guide, and
Father, shall come forth and serve us."

Old Agnes Silverside, the priest's widow, sat with
her hands clasped, and her eyes fixed on the preacher.
As he ended, she laid her hand upon Rose Allen's.

"My maid," she said, "never mind the wilderness;
The stones be sharp, and the sun scorching, and the
thirst sore : but one sight of the King in the Golden
City shall make up for all! "

CHAPTER XI

UNEXPECTED LODGINGS.

OW then, who goes home?" cried the cheerful voice of Mrs. Wade, when the sermon was over. "You, Mistress Benold?—you, Alice Mount?—you, Meg Thurston? You'd best hap your mantle well about your head, Mistress Silverside, this sharp even: you hood of yours is not so thick, and you are not so young as you were once. Now, Adrian Purcas, thee be off with Johnson and Mount; thou'rt not for my money. Agnes Love, woman, I wonder at you! coming out of a November night with no thicker a mantle than that old purple thing, that I'm fair tired of seeing on you. What's that? 'Can't afford a new one?' Go to Southampton! There's one in my coffer that I never use now. Here, Doll! wherever is that lazy bones? Gather up thy heels, wilt thou, and run to my great oak coffer, and bring yon brown hood I set aside. Now don't go and fetch the red one! that's my best Sunday gear, and thou'rt as like to bring red when I tell thee brown as thou art to eat thy supper.—Well, Alice?"

"I cry you mercy, Hostess, for troubling of you; but Master and me, we're bidden to lie at the mill. Mistress Ewring's been that good; but there's no room for Rose, and——"

"Then Rose can turn in with Dorothy, and I'm fain

on't if she'll give her a bit of her earnestness for pay.
There's not as much lead to her heels in a twelvemonth
as would last Doll a week.—So this is what thou calls a
brown hood, is it? I call it a blue apron. Gramercy,
the stupidness o' some folks!"

"Please you, Mistress, there was nought but that in
the coffer."

"What coffer?"

"The walnut, in the porch chamber."

"Well, if ever I did! I never spake a word of the
walnut coffer, nor the porch chamber neither, I told
thee the great oak coffer, and that's in my chamber, as
thou knows, as well as thou knows thy name's Dorothy.
Put that apron back where thou found it, and bring me
the brown hood from the oak coffer. Dear heart, but
she'll go and cast her eyes about for an oak hood in a
brown coffer, as like as not! She's that heedless. It's
not for lack of wit; she could if she would.—Why,
what's to be done with yon little scraps! You can never
get home to Thorpe such a night as this. Johnson! you
leave these bits o' children with me, and I'll send them
back to you to-morrow when the cart goes your way for
a load of malt. There's room enough for you; you'd
all pack in a thimble, well-nigh.—Nay, now! hast thou
really found it? Now then, Agnes Love, cast that over
you, and hap it close to keep you warm. Pay! bless
the woman, I want no pay! only some day I'd like to
hear 'Inasmuch' said to me. Good even!"

"You'll hear that, Mistress Wade!" said Agnes Love,
a pale quiet-looking woman, with a warm grasp of Mistress Wade's hand. "You'll hear that, and something
else, belike—as we've heard to-night, the King will come
forth and serve you. Eh, but it warms one's heart to
hear tell of it!"

"Ay, it doth, dear heart, it doth! Good-night, and

God bless thee! Now, Master Pulleyne, I'll show you your chamber, an' it like you. Rose Allen, you know the way to Dorothy's loft? Well, go you up, and take the little ones with you. It's time for babes like them to be abed. Doll will show you how to make up a bed for them. Art waiting for some one, Bessy?"

"No, Mistress Wade," said Elizabeth Foulkes, who had stood quietly in a corner as though she were; "but if you'd kindly allow it, I'd fain go up too and have a chat with Rose. My mistress gave me leave for another hour yet."

"Hie thee up, good maid, and so do," replied Mrs. Wade cheerily, taking up a candlestick to light Mr. Pulleyne to the room prepared for him, where, as she knew from past experience, he was very likely to sit at study till far into the night.

Dorothy lighted another candle, and offered it to Rose.

"See, you'll lack a light," said she.

"Nay, not to find our tongues," answered Rose, smiling.

"Ah, but to put yon children abed. Look you in the closet, Rose, as you go into the loft, and you'll see a mattress and a roll of blankets, with a canvas coverlet. that shall serve them. You'll turn in with me."

"All right, Doll; I thank you."

"You look weary, Doll," said Elizabeth.

"Weary? Eh, but if you dwelt with our mistress, you'd look weary, be sure. She's as good a woman as ever trod shoe-leather, only she's so monstrous sharp. She thinks you can be there and back before you've fair got it inside your head that you're to go. I marvel many a time whether the angels 'll fly fast enough t serve her when she gets to Heaven. Marry come up but they'll have to step out if they do."

Rose laughed, and led the way upstairs, where she had been several times before.

Inns at that time were built like Continental country inns are now, round a square space, with a garden inside, and a high archway for the entrance, so high that a load of hay could pass underneath. There were no inside stairs, but a flight led up to the second storey from the court-yard, and a balcony running all round the house gave access to the bedrooms. Rose, however, went into none of the rooms, but made her way to one corner, where a second steep flight of stairs ran straight up between the walls. These the girls mounted, and at the top entered a low door, which led into a large, low room, lighted by a skylight, and occupied by little furniture. At the further end was a good-sized bed covered with a patchwork quilt, but without any hangings —the absence of these indicating either great poverty or extremely low rank. There was neither drawers, dressing-table, nor washstand. A large chest beside the bed held all Dorothy's possessions, and a leaf-table which would let down was fixed to the wall under a mirror. A form in one corner, and two stools, made up the rest of the furniture. In a corner close to the entrance stood another door, which Rose opened after she had set up the leaf-table and put the candle upon it. Then, with Elizabeth's help, she dragged out a large, thick straw mattress, and the blankets and coverlet of which Dorothy had spoken, and made up the bed in one of the unoccupied corners. A further search revealed a bolster, but no pillows were forthcoming. That did not matter, for they expected none.

"Now then, children, we'll get you into bed," said Rose.

"Will must say his prayers first," said Cissy anxiously.

"Of course. Now, Will, come and say thy prayers, like a good lad."

Will knelt down beside the bed, and did as he was told in a shrill, sing-song voice. Odd prayers they were; but in those days nobody knew any better, and most children were taught to say still queerer things. First came the Lord's Prayer: so far all was right. Then Will repeated the Ten Commandments and the Creed, which are not prayers at all, and finished with this formula:—

> "Matthew, Mark, Luke and John,
> Bless the bed that I lie on:
> Four corners to my bed,
> Four angels at their head;
> One to read, and one to write,
> And one to guard my bed at night.

> "And now I lay me down to sleep,
> I pray that Christ my soul may keep;
> If I should die before I wake,
> I pray that Christ my soul may take;
> Wake I at morn, or wake I never,
> I give my soul to Christ for ever."

After this strange jumble of good things and nonsense, Will jumped into bed, where the baby was already laid. It was Cissy's turn next. Ever since it had been so summarily arranged by Mrs. Wade that the children were to stay the night at the King's Head, Cissy had been looking preternaturally solemn. Now, when she was desired to say her prayers, as a prelude to going to bed, Cissy's lip quivered, and her eyes filled with tears.

"Why, little maid, what ails thee?" asked Rose.

"It's Father," said Cissy, in an unsteady voice. "I don't know however Father will manage without me. He'll have to dress his own supper. I only hope he'll leave the dish for me to wash when I get home. Nobody never put Father and me asunder afore!"

" Little maid," answered Elizabeth, " Mistress Wade meant to save thee the long walk home."

" Oh, I know she meant it kind," replied Cissy, "and I'm right thankful : but, please, I'd rather be tired than Father be without me. We've never been asunder afore—never ! "

CHAPTER XII.

TRYING ON THE ARMOUR.

"H, thy father 'll do right well!" said Rose encouragingly. "I dare be bound he thought it should be a pleasant change for thee."

"Ay, I dare say Father thought of us and what we should like," said Cissy. "He nodded to Mistress Wade, and smiled on me, as he went forth; so of course I had to 'bide. But then, you see, I'm always thinking of Father."

"I see," said Rose, laughing; "it's not, How shall I do without Father? but, How can Father do without me?"

"That's it," replied Cissy, nodding her capable little head. "He'll do without Will and Baby—not but he'll miss them, you know; but they don't do nothing for him like me."

This was said in Cissy's most demure manner, and Rose was exceedingly amused.

"And, prithee, what dost thou for him?" said she.

"I do everything," said Cissy, with an astonished look. "I light the fire, and dress the meat,[1] and sweep the floor. Only I can't do all the washing yet; Neighbour Ursula has to help me with that. But

---

[1] At this time they used the word *meat* in the sense of food of any kind—not butcher's meat only.

about Father—please, when I've said the Paternoster,[1] and the Belief, and the Commandments, might I ask, think you, for somebody to go in and do things for Father? I know he'll miss me very ill."

"Thou dear little-soul!" cried Rose.

But Cissy was looking up at Elizabeth, whom she dimly discerned to be the graver and wiser of the two girls. Elizabeth smiled at her in that quiet, sweet way which she usually did.

"Little Cissy," she said, "is not God thy Father, and his likewise? And thinkest thou fathers love to see their children happy and at ease, or no?"

"Father likes us to be happy," said Cissy simply.

"And 'your Father knoweth,'" softly replied Elizabeth, "'that ye have need of all these things.'"

"Oh, then, He'll send in Ursula, or somebody," responded Cissy, in a contented tone. "It'll be all right if I ask Him to see to it."

And Cissy "asked Him to see to it," and then lay down peacefully, her tranquillity restored, by the side of little Will, and all the children were asleep in a few minutes.

"Now, Bessy, we can have our talk."

So saying, Rose drew the stools into a corner, out of the way of the wind, which came puffing in at the skylight in a style rather unpleasant for November, and the girls sat down together for a chat.

"How go matters with you at Master Clere's, Bessy?"

"Oh, middling. I go not about to complain, only that I would Mistress Amy were a bit steadier than she is."

"She's a gadabout, isn't she?"

---

[1] The Lord's Prayer.

"Nay, I've said all I need, and maybe more than I should."

"Doth Master Clere go now to mass, Bessy?"

"Oh, ay, as regular as any man in the town, and the mistress belike. The net's drawing closer, Rose. The time will soon come when even you and I, low down as we are, shall have to make choice, with death at the end of one way."

"Ay, I'm afeard so," said Rose gravely. "Bessy, think you that you can stand firm?"

"Firm as a rock, if God hold me up; weak and shifting as water, if He hold me not."

"Ay, thou hast there the right. But we are only weak, ignorant maidens, Bessy."

"Then is He the more likely to hold us up, since He shall see we need it rather. If thou be high up on the rock, out of reach of the waves, what matter whether thou be a stone weight or a crystal vessel? The waters beat upon the rock, not on thee."

"But one sees them coming, Bess."

"Well, what if thou dost? They'll not touch thee."

"Eh, Bess, the fire 'll touch us, be sure!"

"It'll touch our flesh—the outward case of us—that which can drop off and turn to dust. It can never meddle with Rose Allen and Elizabeth Foulkes.

"Bessy, I wish I had thy good courage."

"Why, Rose, art feared of death?"

"Not of what comes after, thank God! But I'm feared of pain, Bessy, and of dying. It seems so shocking, when one looks foward to it."

"Best not look forward. Maybe 'tis more shocking to think of than to feel. That's the way with many things."

"O Bessy! I can't look on it calm, like that. It isn't nature."

"Nay, dear heart, 'tis grace, not nature."

And thou seest, in one way, 'tis worser for me than for thee. Thou art thyself alone; but there's Father and Mother with me. How could I bear to see them suffer?"

"The Lord will never call thee to anything, Rose, which He will not give thee grace to bear. Be sure of that. Well, I've no father—he's in Heaven, long years ago. But I've a good mother at Stoke Nayland, and I'd sooner hurt my own head than her little finger, any day I live. Dear maid, neither thou nor I know to what the Lord will call us. We do but know that on whatever journey He sendeth us, Himself shall pay the charges. Thou goest not a warfare at thine own cost. How many times in God's Word is it said, 'Fear not?' Would the Lord have so oft repeated it, without He had known that we were very apt to fear?"

"Ah!" said Rose, sighing, "and the 'fearful' be among such as are left without the gate. O Bessy, if that fear should overcome me that I draw back! I cannot but think every moment shall make it more terrible to bear. And if one held not fast, but bought life, as soon as the fire were felt, by denying the truth! I am feared, dear heart! I'm feared."

"It shall do thee no hurt to be feared of thyself. only lose not thine hold on God. 'Hold *Thou* me up, and I shall be safe.' But that should not be, buying life, Bessy, but selling it."

"I know it should be bartering the life eternal, for the sake of a few years, at most, of this lower life. Yet life is main sweet, Bessy, and we are young. 'All that a man hath will he give for his life.'"

"Think not on the life, Rose, nor on what thou givest, but alone on Him for whom thou givest it. Is He not worth the pain and the loss? Couldst thou

bear to lose *Him?*—Him, who endured the bitter
rood [1] rather than lose thee.   That must never be,
dear heart."

"I do trust not, verily ; yet——"

"What, not abed yet?" cried the cheery voice of
Mrs. Wade. "I came up but to see if you had all
you lacked. Doll's on her way up. I reckon she
shall be here by morning.   A good maid, surely, but
main slow. What! the little ones be asleep? That's
well.   But, deary me, what long faces have you two!
Are you taking thought for your funeral, or what dis-
course have you, that you both look like judges?"

"Something like it, Hostess," said Elizabeth, with
her grave smile. "Truly, we were considering that
which may come, and marvelling if we should hold fast."

The landlady set her arms akimbo, and looked from
one of the girls to the other.

"Why, what's a-coming?" said she.

"Nay, we know not what, but——"

"Dear heart, then I'd wait till I did! I'll tell you
what it is—I hate to have things wasted, even an old
shoe-latchet; why, I pity to cast it aside, lest it should
come in for something some day. Now, my good maids,
don't waste your courage and resolution.   Just you
keep them till they're wanted, and then they'll be
bright and ready for use. You're not going to be
burned to-night; you're going to bed.   And screwing
up your courage to be burned is an ill preparation for
going to bed, I can tell you. You don't know, and I
don't, that any one of us will be called to glorify the
Lord in the fires.   If we are, depend upon it He'll show
us how to do it.   Now, then, say your prayers, and go
to sleep."

---

[1] Cross.

" I thank you, Hostess, but I must be going home."

" Good-night, then, Bessy, and don't sing funeral dirges over your own coffin afore it comes from the undertaker. What, Doll, hast really got here ? I scarce looked to see thee afore morning. Good-night, maids."

And Mrs. Wade bustled away.

CHAPTER XIII

A DARK NIGHT'S ERRAND.

"JUST you be gone, Bessy?" said Dorothy Denny, sitting down on the side of her bed with a weary air. "Eh, I'm proper tired! Thought this day'd never come to an end, I did. Couldn't you tarry a bit longer?"

"I don't think I ought, Dorothy. Your mistress looked to see Rose abed by now, 'twas plain; and mine gave me leave but till eight o' the clock. I'd better be on my way."

"Oh, you're one of that sort that's always thinking what they *ought*, are you? That's all very well in the main; but, dear heart! one wants a bit of what one would like by nows and thens."

"One gets that best by thinking what one ought," said Elizabeth.

"Ay, but it's all to come sometime a long way off; and how do I know it'll come to me? Great folks doesn't take so much note of poor ones, and them above 'll very like do so too."

"There's only One above that has any right to bid aught," answered Elizabeth, "and He takes more note of poor than rich, Doll, as you'll find by the Bible. Good-night, Rose; good-night, Dorothy."

And Elizabeth ran lightly down the stairs, and out

into the street. She had a few minutes left before the hour at which Mrs. Clere had enjoined her to be back, so she did not need to hurry, and she went quietly on towards Balcon Lane, carrying her lantern—for there were no street lamps, and nobody could have any light on a winter evening except what he carried with him. Just before she turned the corner of the lane she met two women, both rather heavily laden. Elizabeth was passing on, when her steps were arrested by hearing one of them say,—

" I do believe that's Bess Foulkes; and if it be——"
Elizabeth came to a standstill.

" Yes, I'm Bess Foulkes," she said.   " What of that ? "

" Why, then, you'll give me a lift, be sure, as far as the North Hill.   I've got more than I can carry, and I was casting about for a face I knew."

" I've not much time to spare," said Elizabeth ; " but I'll give you a lift as far as St. Peter's—I can't go further.   Margaret Thurston, isn't it ?   I must be in by eight ; I'll go with you till then."

" I've only to go four doors past St. Peter's, so that'll do well.   You were at the preaching, weren't you, this even ? "

" Ay, and I thought I saw you."

" Yes, I was there.   He talked full bravely.   I marvel if he'd stand if it came to it.   I don't think many would."

" I misdoubt if any would, without God held them up."

" Margaret says she's sure she would," said the other woman.

" Oh, ay, I don't doubt myself," said Margaret.

" Then I cry you mercy, but I doubt you," replied Elizabeth.

"I'm sure you needn't! I'd never flinch for pope nor priest."

"Maybe not; but you might for rack or stake."

"It'll ne'er come to that here. Queen Mary's not like to forget how Colchester folk all stood with her against Lady Jane."

"She mayn't; but think you the priests shall tarry at that? and she'll do as the priests bid her."

"Ay, they say my Lord of Winchester, when he lived, had but to hold up his finger, and she'd have followed him, if it were over London Bridge into the Thames," said the other woman. "And the like with my Lord Cardinal, that now is."

By "my Lord of Winchester" she meant Bishop Gardiner, who had been dead rather more than a year. The Cardinal was Reginald Pole, the Queen's third cousin, who had lately been appointed Archbishop of Canterbury, in the room of the martyred Cranmer.

"Why, the Queen and my Lord Cardinal were ever friends, from the time they were little children," answered Margaret.

"Ay, there was talk once of her wedding with him, if he'd not become a priest. But I rather reckon you're right, my maid: a priest's a priest, without he's a Gospeller; and there's few of them will think more of goodness and charity than of their own order and of the Church."

"Goodness and charity? Marry, there's none in 'em!" cried Margaret. "Howbeit, here's the Green Sleeves, where I'm bound, and I'm beholden to you, Bessy, for coming with me. Good even."

Elizabeth returned the greeting, and set off to walk back at a quick pace to Balcon Lane. She had not gone many steps when she was once more stopped, this time by a young man, named Robert Purcas, a fuller, who lived in the neighbouring village of Bocking.

"Bessy," said he. "It is thou, I know well, for I heard thee bid Margaret Thurston good den, and I should know thy voice among a thousand."

"I cannot 'bide, Robin. I'm late, even now."

"Tarry but one minute, Bessy. Trust me, thou wouldst if——"

"Well, then, make haste," said Elizabeth, pausing.

"Thou art friends with Alice Mount, of Bentley, and she knows Mistress Ewring, the miller's wife."

"Ay; well, what so?"

"Bid Alice Mount tell Master Ewring there's like to be a writ out against him for heresy and contumaciousness toward the Church. Never mind how I got to know; I know it, and that's enough. He, and Mistress Silverside, and Johnson, of Thorpe, be like enough to come into court. Bessy, take heed to thy ways, I pray thee, that thou be not suspect."

No thought of herself had caused Elizabeth Foulkes to lay her hand suddenly on the buttress of St. Peter's, beside her. The father who was so dear to little Cissy was in imminent danger; and Cissy had just been asking God to send somebody to see after him. Elizabeth's voice was changed when she spoke again."

"They must be warned," she said. "Robin, thou and I must needs do this errand to-night. I shall be chidden, but that does not matter. Canst thou walk ten miles for the love of God?"

"I'd do that for the love of thee, never name God."

Elizabeth did not answer the words. There was too much at stake to lose time.

"Then go thou to Thorpe, and bid Johnson get away ere they take him. Mistress Wade has the children, and she'll see to them, or Alice Mount will. I must——"

"Thou'd best not put too much on Alice Mount, for Will Mount's as like as not to be in tho next batch."

"Lord, have mercy on us! I'll go warn them—they are with Mistress Ewring at the mill; and then I'll go on to Mistress Silverside. Make haste, Robin, for mercy's sake!"

And, without waiting for anything more, Elizabeth turned and ran up the street as fast as she dared in the comparative darkness. Streets were very rough in those days, and lanterns would not light far.

Old Mistress Silverside lived in Tenant's Lane, which was further off than the mill. Elizabeth ran across from the North Hill to Boucher's Street, and up that, towards the gate, beyond which the mill stood on the bank of the Colne. Mr. Ewring, the miller, was a man who kept early hours; and, as Elizabeth ran up to the gate, she saw that the lights were already out in the windows of the mill. The gate was closed. Elizabeth rapped sharply on the window, and the shutter was opened, but, all being dark inside, she could not see by whom.

"Prithee, let me through the gate. I've a message of import for Master Ewring, at the mill."

"Gate's shut," said the gruff voice of the gate-keeper. "Can't let any through while morning."

"Darnell, you'll let me through!" pleaded Elizabeth. "I'm servant to Master Clere, clothier, of Balcon Lane, and I'm sent with a message of grave import to the mill."

"Tell Master Clere, if he wants his corn ground, he must send by daylight."

And the wooden shutter was flung to. Elizabeth stood for an instant as if dazed.

"I can't get to them," she said to herself. "There's no chance that way. I must go to Tenant's Lane."

She turned away from the gate, and went round by the wall to the top of Tenant's Lane.

"Pray God I be in time to warn somebody! We are all in danger, we who were at the preaching to-night, and Mistress Wade most of all, for it was in her house. I'll go to the King's Head ere I go home."

Thus thinking, Elizabeth reached Mrs. Silverside's, and rapped at the door. Once—twice—thrice—four times. Not a sound came from inside, and she was at last sorrowfully compelled to conclude that nobody was at home. Down the lane she went, and came out into High Street at the bottom.

"Then I can only warn Mistress Wade. I dare be bound she'll let the others know, as soon as morning breaks. I do trust that will be time enough."

She picked her way across High Street, and had just reached the opposite side, when her arm was caught as if in an iron vice, and she felt herself held fast by greater strength than her own.

"Hussy, what goest thou about?" said the stern voice of her master, Nicholas Clere.

CHAPTER XIV

ICHOLAS CLERE was a man of one idea at once; and people of that sort do a great deal of good when they get hold of the right idea, and a great deal of harm when a wrong idea gets hold of them. Once let a notion get into the head of Nicholas, and no reasoning nor persuasion would drive it out. He made no allowances and permitted no excuses. If a thing looked wrong, then wrong it must be, and it was of no use to talk to him about it. That he should have found Elizabeth, who had been ordered to come home at eight o'clock, running in the opposite direction at half-past eight, was in his eyes an enormity which admitted of no explanations. That she either had been in mischief, or was then on her way to it, were the only two alternatives possible to the mind of her master.

And circumstances were especially awkward for Elizabeth, since she could not give any explanation of her proceedings which would clear her in the eyes of her employers. Nicholas Clere, like many other people of prejudiced minds and fixed opinions, had a mind totally unfixed in the one matter of religion. His religion was whatever he found it to his worldly advantage to be. During King Edward's reign, it was polite and fashionable to be a Protestant; now, under Queen

Mary, the only way to make a man's fortune was to be
a Roman Catholic. And though Nicholas did not say
even to himself that it was better to have plenty of
money than to go to Heaven when he died, yet he lived
exactly as if he thought so. During the last few years,
therefore, Nicholas had gradually been growing more
and more of a Papist, and especially during the last few
weeks. First, he left off attending the Protestant
meetings at the King's Head; then he dropped family
prayer. Papists, whether they be the genuine article
or only the imitation, always dislike family prayer. They
say that a church is the proper place to pray in, though
our Lord's bidding is, "When thou prayest, enter into
thy closet, and when thou hast shut thy door, pray to
thy Father which is in secret." The third step which
Nicholas took was to go to mass, and command all his
household to follow him. This had Elizabeth hitherto,
but quite respectfully, declined to do. She was ready
to obey all orders of her earthly master which did not
interfere with her higher duty to God Almighty. But
His holy Word—not her fancy, nor the traditions of
men—forbade her to bow down to graven images; or to
give His glory to any person or thing but Himself.
And Elizabeth knew that she could not attend mass
without doing that. A piece of consecrated bread
would be held up, and she would be required to worship
it as God. And it was not God: it could neither see,
nor hear, nor speak; it was not even as like God as a
man is. To worship a bit of bread because Christ
likened His body to bread, would be as silly as to
worship a stone because the Bible says, "That *Rock*
was Christ." It was evident that He was speaking
figuratively, just as He spoke when He said, "I am
the door of the sheep," and "I am the Morning
Star." Who in his senses would suppose that Christ

meant to say that He was a wooden door? It is important that we should have true ideas about this, because there are just now plenty of foolish people who will try to persuade us to believe that that poor, powerless piece of bread is God Himself. It is insulting the Lord God Almighty to say such a thing. Look at the 115th Psalm, from the fifth verse to the eight, and you will see how God describes an idol, which He forbids to be worshipped: and then look at the 26th and 27th verses of the 24th chapter of St. Matthew, and you will see that the Lord Jesus distinctly says that you are not to believe anybody who tells you that He is come before you see Him. When He really does come, nobody will want any telling; we shall all see Him for ourselves. So we find from His own words in every way that the bread and wine in the Sacrament are just bread and wine, and nothing more, which we eat and drink "in remembrance of Him," just as you might keep and value your mother's photograph in remembrance of her. But I am sure you never would be so silly as to think that the photograph was her own real self!

This was the reason why Elizabeth Foulkes would not go to mass. Every Sunday morning Mrs. Clere ordered her to go, and Elizabeth quietly, respectfully, but firmly, told her that she could not do so. Elizabeth had God's Word to uphold her; God forbade her to worship idols. It was not simply that she did not like it, nor that somebody else had told her not to do it. Nothing can excuse us if we break the laws of our country, unless the law of our country has broken God's law; and Elizabeth would have done very wrong to disobey her mistress, except when her mistress told her to disobey God. What God said must be her rule; not what she thought.

Generally speaking, Mrs. Clere called Elizabeth some ugly names, and then let her do as she liked. Up to this time her master had not interfered with her, but she was constantly expecting that he would. She was not afraid of answering for herself; but she was terribly afraid for her poor friends. To tell him that she was on her way to warn them of danger, and beg them to escape, would be the very means of preventing their escape, for what he was likely to do was to go at once and tell the priests, in order to win their favour for himself.

"Hussy, what goest thou about?" came sternly from Nicholas Clere, as he held her fast.

"Master, I cry you mercy. I was on my way home, and I was turned out of it by one that prayed me to take a word of grave import to a friend."

Elizabeth thought she might safely say so much as that.

"I believe thee not," answered Nicholas. "All young maids be idle gadabouts, if they be not looked to sharply, and thou art no better than the rest. Whither wert thou going?"

"I have told all I may, Master, and I pray you ask no further. The secret is not mine, but theirs that sent me and should have received my message."

In those days, nothing was more usual than for secret messages to be sent from one person to another. It was not safe then, as it is now, for people to speak openly. Freedom always goes hand in hand with Protestantism. If England should ever again become a Roman Catholic country—which many people are trying hard to make her—Englishmen will be no longer free.

Nicholas Clere hesitated a moment. Elizabeth's defence was not at all unlikely to be true. But he had

made up his mind that she was in fault, and probabili-
ties must not be allowed to interfere with it.

"Rubbish!" said he. "What man, having his eyes
in his head, should trust a silly maid with any matter
of import? Women can never keep a secret, much less
a young jade like to thee. Tell no more lies, prithee."

And he began to walk towards Balcon Lane, still
firmly holding Elizabeth by the arm.

"Master, I beseech you, let me go on my way!" she
pleaded earnestly. "I will tarry up all night, if it be
your pleasure, to make up for one half-hour now. Truly
as I am an honest maid, I have told you the truth, and
I am about nothing ill."

"Tush, jade! Hold thy tongue. Thou goest with
me, and if not peaceably, then by force."

"Will you, of your grace, Master, let me leave my
message with some other to take instead of me? May
I have leave to speak, but one moment, with Mistress
Wade, of the King's Head? She would find a trusty
messenger to go forward."

"Tell me thy message, and if it be truly of any
weight, then shall it be sent," answered Nicholas, still
coldly, but less angrily than before.

Could she tell him the message? Would it not go
straight to the priest, and all hope of escape be thus cut
off? Like Nehemiah, Elizabeth cried for wisdom.

"Master, I cry you mercy yet again, but I may not
tell the message."

"Yet thou wouldst fain tell Mistress Wade! Thou
wicked hussy, thou canst be after no good. What
message is this, which thou canst tell Mistress Wade,
but mayest not tell me? I crede thee not a word.
Have forward, and thy mistress shall deal with thee."

CHAPTER XV

SILENCE UNDER DIFFICULTIES.

LIZABETH FOULKES was almost in despair. Her master held her arm tight, and he was a strong man—to break away from him was simply impossible—and to persuade him to release her seemed about as unlikely. Still she cried, "Master, let me go!" in tones that might have melted any softer heart than that of Nicholas Clere.

"Step out!" was all he said, as he compelled Elizabeth to keep pace with him till they reached Balcon Lane. Mrs. Clere was busy in the kitchen. She stopped short as they entered, with a gridiron in her hand which she had cleaned and was about to hang up.

"Well, this is a proper time of night to come home, mistress! Marched in, too, with thy master holding of thee, as if the constable had thee in custody! This is our pious maid, that can talk nought but Bible, and says her prayers once a day oftener nor other folks! I always do think that sort no better than hypocrites. What hath she been about, Nicholas? what saith she?"

"A pack o' lies!" said Nicholas, harshly. "Whined out a tale of some message of dread import that somebody, that must not be named, hath sent her on. I found her hasting with all speed across the High Street, the contrary way from what it should have been. You'd best give her the strap, wife. She deserves it, or will ere long."

Nicholas sat down in the chimney-corner, leaving Mistress Clere to deal with the offender. Elizabeth well knew that the strap was no figure of speech, and that Mistress Clere when angry had no light hand. Girls were beaten cruelly in those days, and grown women too, when their mothers or mistresses chose to punish them for real or supposed offences. But Elizabeth Foulkes thought very little of the pain she might suffer, and very much of the needed warning which had not been given. And then, suddenly, the words flashed across her, "Thy will be done on earth, as it is in Heaven." Then the warning was better let alone, if it were God's will. She rose with a calmer face, and followed Mistress Clere to the next room to receive her penalty.

"There!" said that lady, when her arm began to ache with beating Elizabeth. "That'll do for a bit, I hope. Perhaps thou'lt not be so headstrong next time. I vow, she looks as sweet as if I'd given her a box of sugar plums! I'm feared thou'd have done with a bit more, but I'm proper tired. Now, speak the truth: who sent thee on this wild-goose chase?"

"Mistress, I was trusted with a secret. Pray you, ask me not."

"Secret me no secrets! I'll have it forth."

"Not of me," said Elizabeth, quietly, but firmly.

"Highty-tighty! and who art thou, my lady?"

"I am your servant, mistress, and will do your bidding in everything that toucheth not my duty to God Almighty. But this I cannot."

"I'll tell thee what, hussy! it was never good world since folks set up to think for themselves what was right and wrong, instead of hearkening to the priest, and doing as they were bid. Thou'rt too proud, Bess

Foulkes, that's where it is, with thy pretty face and
thy dainty ways. Go thou up and get thee abed—it's
on the stroke of nine : and I'll come and lock thee in.
Dear heart, to see the masterfulness of these maids!"

"Mistress," said Elizabeth, pausing, "I pray you
reckon me not disobedient, for in very deed I have ever
obeyed you, and yet will, touching all concerns of yours:
but under your good leave, this matter concerns you
not, and I have no freedom to speak thereof."

"In very deed, my lady," said Mistress Clere, dropping a mock courtesy, "I desire not to meddle with
your ladyship's high matters of state, and do intreat
you of pardon that I took upon me so weighty a matter.
Go get thee abed, hussy, and hold thine idle tongue!"

Elizabeth turned and went upstairs in silence. Words
were of no use. Mistress Clere followed her. In the
bedroom where they both slept, which was a loft with a
skylight, was Amy, half undressed, and employed in
her customary but very unnecessary luxury of admiring
herself in the glass.

"Amy, I'm going to turn the key. Here's an ill
maid that I've had to take the strap to : see thou fall
not in her ways. I'll let you out in the morning."

So saying, Mistress Clere locked the door, and left
the two girls together.

Like most idle folks, Amy Clere was gifted with her
full share of curiosity. The people who do the world's
work, or who go about doing good, are not usually the
people who want you to tell them how much Miss Smith
gave for her new bonnet, or whom Mr. Robinson had
yesterday to dinner. They are a great deal too busy,
and generally too happy, to give themselves the least trouble about the bonnet, or to feel the slightest interest in the
dinner-party. But idle people—poor pitiable things !—
who do not know what to do with themselves, are often

very ready to discuss anything of that sort which considerately puts itself in their way. To have something to talk about is both a surprise and a delight to them.

No sooner had Mrs. Clere shut the door than Amy dropped her edifying occupation and came up to Elizabeth, who had sat wearily down on the side of the bed.

"Why, Bess, what ails Mother? and what hast thou been doing? Thou mayest tell me; I'll not make no mischief, and I'd love dearly to hear all about it."

If experience had assured Elizabeth Foulkes of anything, it was that she might as safely repeat a narrative to the town-crier as tell it to Amy Clere.

"I have offenced Mistress," said she, "and I am sorry thereat: yet I did but what I thought was my duty. I can say no more thereanent, Mistress Amy."

"But what didst thou, Bessy? Do tell me."

Elizabeth shook her head. "Best not, Mistress Amy. Leave it rest, I pray you, and me likewise, for of a truth I am sore wearied."

"Come, Bessy, don't be grumpy! let's know what it was. Life's monstrous tiresome, and never a bit of play nor show. I want to know all about it."

"Maybe there'll be shows ere long for you, Mistress Amy," answered Elizabeth gravely, as a cold shiver ran through her to think of what might be the consequence of her untold message. Well! Cissy's father at any rate would be safe : thank God for that!

"Why will there? Hast been at one to-night?"

"No." Elizabeth checked herself from saying more. What a difference there was between Amy's fancies and the stern realities she knew!

"There's no lugging nought out of thee!" said Amy with a pout. "Thou'rt as close shut as an oyster shell."

And she went back to the mirror, and began to plait her hair, the more conveniently to tuck it under her night-cap. Oh, how Elizabeth longed for a safe confidant that night! Sometimes she felt as though she must pour out her knowledge and her fears—to Amy, if she could get no one else. But she knew too well that, without any evil intention, Amy would be certain to make mischief from sheer love of gossip, the moment she met with any one who would listen to her.

"Mistress Amy, I'm right weary. Pray you, leave me be."

"Hold thy tongue if thou wilt. I want nought with thee, not I," replied Amy, with equal crossness and untruth, since, as she would herself have expressed it, she was dying to know what Elizabeth could have done to make her mother so angry. But Amy was angry herself now. "Get thee abed, Mistress Glum-face; I'll pay thee out some day: see if I don't!"

Elizabeth's reply was to kneel down for prayer. There was one safe Confidant, who could be relied upon for sympathy and secrecy: and He might be spoken to without words. It was well; for the words refused to come. Only one thing would present itself to Elizabeth's weary heart and brain: and that was the speech of little Cissy, that, "it would be all right if she asked God to see to it." A sob broke from her, as she sent up to Heaven the one petition of which alone she felt capable just then—"Lord, help me!" He would know how and when to help. Elizabeth dropped her trouble into the Almighty hands, and left it there. Then she rose, undressed, and lay down beside Amy, who was already in bed.

Amy Clere was not an ill-natured girl, and her anger never lasted long. When she heard Elizabeth's sob, her heart smote her a little: but she said to herself, that she was "not going to humble herself to that crusty Bess," so she turned round and went to sleep.

CHAPTER XVI.

THE STORM BREAKS.

HEN the morning came, Amy's good temper was restored by her night's rest. and she was inclined to look on her locking-in as a peice of amusement.

"I vow, Bess, this is fun!" said she, "I've twenty minds to get out on the roof, and see if I can reach the next window. It would be right jolly to wake up Ellen Mallory—she's always lies abed while seven; and I do think I could. Wilt aid me?"

Ellen Mallory was the next neighbour's daughter, a girl of about Amy's age; and seven o'clock was considered a shocking late hour for rising in 1556.

"Mistress Amy, I do pray you never think of such a thing," cried Elizabeth, in horror. "You'll be killed!"

"Well, I'm not wishful to be killed," answered Amy lightly: "I only want some fun while we are shut up here. I marvel when Mother shall come to let us out. She'll have to light the fire herself if she does not; that's one good thing!"

Elizabeth thought it a very undutiful idea; but she was silent. If she had but had wings like a dove, how gladly would she have flown to warn her friends! She well knew that Mrs. Clere was not likely to be in the mood to grant a favour and let her go, after what had happened the night before. To go without leave was a thing which Elizabeth never contemplated. That would be putting herself in the wrong. But her poor friends, would they escape? How if Robert Purcas had been stopped, as she had? I was strange, but her imagination did not dwell nearly so much upon her own friend, Rose, as on little Cissy. If Johnson were taken, if he were martyred, what would become of little Cissy? The child had crept into Elizabeth's heart, before she was aware. Suddenly Amy's voice broke in upon her thoughts.

"Come, Bess, art in a better mood this morrow? I'll forgive thee thy miss-words last night, if thou'lt tell me now."

All the cross words there had been the night before had come from Amy herself; but Elizabeth let that pass.

"Mistress Amy," said she, "this matter is not one whereof I may speak to you or any other. I was charged with a secret, and bidden not to disclose the same. Think you I can break my word?"

"Dear heart! I break mine many a time in the week," cried Amy, with a laugh. "I'm not nigh so peevish as thou."

"But, Mistress Amy, it is not right," returned Elizabeth earnestly.

Before Amy could answer, Mrs. Clere's heavy step was heard approaching the door, and the key turned in the lock. Amy, who sat on the side of the bed swinging her feet to and fro for amusement, jumped down.

"Mother, you'll get nought from her. I've essayed both last night and this morrow, and I might as well have held my tongue."

"Go and light the fire," said Mrs. Clere sternly to Elizabeth. "I'll have some talk with thee at after."

Elizabeth obeyed in silence. She lighted the fire,

and buttered the eggs, and swept the house, and baked the bread, and washed the clothes, and churned the butter—all with a passionate longing to be free, hidden in her heart, and constant ejaculatory prayers—silent ones, of course—for the safety of her poor friends. Mrs. Clere seemed to expect Elizabeth to run away if she could, and she did not let her go out of her sight the whole day. The promised scolding, however, did not come.

Supper was over, and the short winter day was drawing to its close, when Nicholas Clere came into the kitchen.

"Here's brave news, Wife!" said he, "What thinkest? Here be an half-dozen in the town arrest of heresy—and some without, too."

"Mercy on us! Who?" demanded Mrs. Clere.

"Why, Master Benold, chandler, and Master Bongeor, glazier, and old Mistress Silverside, and Mistress Ewring at the mill—these did I hear. I know not who else." And suddenly turning to Elizabeth, he said, "Hussy, was this thine errand, or had it ought to do therewith?"

All the passionate pain and the earnest longing died out of the heart of Elizabeth Foulkes. She stood looking as calm as a marble statue, and almost as white.

"Master," she said, quietly enough, "mine errand was to warn these my friends. God may yet save them, if it be His will. And may He not lay to your charge the blood that will otherwise be shed!"

"Mercy on us!" cried Mrs. Clere again, dropping her duster. "Why, the jade's never a bit better than these precious friends of hers!"

"I'm sore afeared we have been nourishing a serpent in our bosoms," said Nicholas, in his sternest manner. "I had best see to this."

"Well, I wouldn't hurt the maid," said his wife, in an uneasy tone; "but, dear heart! we must see to ourselves a bit. We shall get into trouble if such things be tracked to our house."

"So we shall," answered her husband. "I shall go, speak with the priest, and see what he saith. Without"—and he turned to Elizabeth—"thou wilt be penitent, and go to mass, and do penance for thy fault."

"I am willing enough to do penance for my faults, Master," said Elizabeth, "but not for the warning that I would have given; for no fault is in it."

"Then must we need save ourselves," replied Nicholas: "for the innocent must not suffer for the guilty. Wife, thou wert best lock up this hussy in some safe place; and, daughter, go thou not nigh her. This manner of heresy is infectious, and I would not have thee defiled therewith."

"Nay, I'll have nought to do with what might get me into trouble," said Amy, flippantly. "Bessy may swallow the Bible if she likes; I shan't."

Elizabeth was silent, quietly standing to hear her doom pronounced. She knew it was equivalent to a sentence of death. No priest, consulted on such a subject would dare to leave the heretic undenounced. And she had no friends save that widowed mother at Stoke Nayland—a poor woman, without money or influence; and that other Friend who would be sure to stand by her,—who, that He might save others, had not saved Himself.

Nicholas took up his hat and marched out, and Mrs. Clere ordered Elizabeth off to a little room over the porch, generally used as a lumber room, where she locked her up.

"Now then, think on thy ways!" said she. "It'll

mayhap do thee good. Bread and water's all thou'lt
get, I promise thee, and better than thy demerits.
Dear heart! to turn a tidy house upside-down like this,
and all for a silly maid's fancies, forsooth! I hope thou
feels ashamed of thyself; for I do for thee."

"Mistress, I can never be ashamed of God's truth.
To that will I stand, if He grant me grace."

"Have done with thy cant! I've no patience with
it."

And Mistress Clere banged the door behind her,
locked it, and left Elizabeth alone till dinner-time,
when she carried up a slice of bread—only one, and
that the coarsest rye bread—and a mug of water.

"There!" said she. "Thou shouldst be thankful,
when I've every bit of work on my hands in all this
house, owing to thy perversity!"

"I do thank you, Mistress," said Elizabeth, meekly.
"Would you suffer me to ask you one favour? I
have served you well hitherto, and I never disobeyed
you till now."

It was true, and Mrs. Clere knew it.

"Well, the brazenfacedness of some hussies!" cried
she. "Prithee, what's your pleasure, mistress? Would
you a new satin gown for your trial, and a pearl-neck-
lace? or do you desire an hundred pounds given to the
judges to set you free? or would you a petition to the
Queen's Majesty, headed by Mr. Mayor and my Lord of
Oxenford?"

Elizabeth let the taunts go by her like a summer
breeze. She felt them keenly enough. Nobody enjoys
being laughed at; but he is hardly worth calling a man
who allows a laugh to turn him out of the path of
duty.

"Mistress," she said, quietly, "should you hear of
any being arrested for heresy, would you do me so much

grace as to let me know the name ? and the like if you hear of any that have escaped ? "

Mrs. Clere looked down into the eyes that were lifted to her, as Elizabeth stood before her. Quiet, meek, tranquil eyes, without a look of reproach in them, with no anxiety save that aroused for the fate of her friends. She was touched in spite of herself.

" Thou foolish maid ! " said she. " Why couldst thou not have done as other folks, and run no risks? I vow I'm well-nigh sorry for thee, for all thy perversity. Well, we'll see. Mayhap I will, if I think on't."

" Thank you, Mistress ! " said Elizabeth gratefully, as Mistress Clere took the mug from her, and left the little porch chamber as before, locking her prisoner in the prison.

CHAPTER XVII.

ROSE HEARS THE NEWS.

HILE Elizabeth Foulkes was passing through these experiences, the Mounts, Rose Allen, and the children, had gone back to Much Bentley as soon as morning broke. Rose took the little ones home to Thorpe, and they met Johnson just at the door of his own cottage.

"Truly, friend, I am much beholden to you," said he to Rose, "for your kindly care of my little ones. But, I pray you, is it true what I heard, that Mistress Silverside is arrest for heresy?"

Rose looked up in horrified astonishment.

"Why, we left them right well," she said, "but five hours gone. I brought the children o'er to you so soon as they had had their dinner. Is it true, think you?"

"Nay, that would I fain know of you, that were in town twelve hours later than I," answered Johnson.

"Then, in very deed, we heard nought," said Rose. "I do trust it shall prove but an ill rumour.

"May it be so! yet I cannot but fear it be true. Robin Purcas came to me last night, and I could not but think he should have told me somewhat an' he might: but he found Father Tye in mine house, and might not speak. They both tarried so long," added Johnson, with a laugh, "that I was fain to marvel if each were essaying to outsit the other; but if so, Father Tye won, for Love of the Heath came for Robin and took him away ere the priest were wearied out. If any straitness do arise against the Gospellers, Love had best look out."

"Aye, they know him too well to leave him slip through their fingers again," replied Rose.

"That do they, verily. Well, dear hearts, and have ye been good children?"

"We've tried," said Cissy.

"They've been as good as could be," answered Rose.

"Father, did anybody come and see to you? I asked the Lord to see to it, because I knew you'd miss me sore," said Cissy anxiously, "and I want to know if He did."

"Ay, my dear heart," replied Johnson, smiling as he looked down on her. "Ursula Felstede came in and dressed dinner for me, and Margaret Thurston looked in after, and she washed some matters and did a bit of mending; and at after I had company—Father Tye, and Robin Purcas, and Jack Love. So thou seest I was not right lonesome."

"He took good care of yon, Father," said Cissy, looking happy. It was evident that Cissy lived for and in her father. Whatever he was, for good or evil, that she was likewise.

"Well, I've got to look in on Margaret Thurston," said Rose, "for I did a bit of marketing for her this morrow in the town, and I have a fardel to leave. She was not at home when we passed, coming. But now, I think I'd better be on my way, so I'll wish you good den, Johnson. God bless you, little ones!"

"Good den, Rose!" said Cissy. "And you'll learn me to weave lace with those pretty bobbins?"

"That will I, with a very good will, sweet heart," said Rose, stooping to kiss Cissy.

"Weave lace!" commented her father. "What,

G

what is the child thinking, that she would fain learn to weave lace?"

"Oh, Father, please, you won't say nay!" pleaded Cissy, embracing her father's arm with both her own. "I want to bring you in some money." Cissy spoke with a most important air. "You know, of an even, I alway have a bit of time, after Will and Baby be abed, and at times too in the day, when Will's out with George Felstede, and I'm minding Baby; I can rock her with my feet while I make lace with my hands. And you know, Father, Will and Baby 'll be growing big by and bye, and you won't have enough for us all without we do something. And Rose says she'll learn me how, and that if I have a lace pillow—and it won't cost very much, Father!—I can alway take it up for a few minutes by nows and thens, when I have a bit of time, and then, don't you see, Father? I can make a little money for you. Please, *please* don't say I mustn't!" cried Cissy, growing quite talkative in her eagerness.

Johnson and Rose looked at each other, and Rose laughed; but though Cissy's father smiled too, he soon grew grave, and laid his hand on his little girl's head, as she stood looking up earnestly.

"Nay, my little maid, I'll never say nought of the sort. If Rose here will be so good as to learn thee aught that is good, whether for body or soul, I will be truly thankful to her, and bid thee do the like and be diligent to learn. Good little maid! God bless thee!"

Then, as Cissy trotted into the cottage, well pleased, Johnson added, "Bless the little maid's heart! she grows more like her mother in Heaven every day. I'll never stay the little fingers from doing what they can. It'll not bring much in, I reckon, but it'll be a pleasure to the child, and good for her to be ever busy at something, that she mayn't fall into idle ways. Think you not so, Rose?"

"Indeed, and it so will, Johnson," answered Rose; "not that I think Cissy and idle ways 'll ever have much to do one with the other. She's not one of that sort. But I shouldn't wonder if lace-weaving brings in more than you think. I've made a pretty penny of it, and I wasn't so young as Cissy when I learned the work, and it's like everything else—them that begin young have the best chance to make good workers. She'll be a rare comfort to you, Cissy, if she goes on as she's begun."

Johnson did not reply for a moment. When he did, it was to say, "Well, God keep us all! I'm right thankful to you, Rose, for all your goodness to my little maid. Good den!"

When she had returned the "good evening," Rose set off home, and walked rather fast till she came to Margaret Thurston's cottage. After the little business was transacted between her and Margaret, Rose inquired if they had heard of Mistress Silverside's arrest. Both Margaret and her husband seemed thunderstruck.

"Nay, we know nought thereof," answered Thurston. "Pray God it be not true! There'll be more an' it so be."

"I fear so much," said Rose.

She did not tell her mother, for Alice had not been well lately, and Rose wished to spare her an apprehension which might turn out to be quite unfounded, or at least exaggerated. But she told her stepfather, and old Mount looked very grave.

"God grant it be not so!" said he. "But if it be, Rose, thou wist they have our names in their black list of heretics."

"Aye, Father, I know they have."

"God keep us all!" said William Mount, looking earnestly into the fire.

And Rose knew that while he might intend to include

being kept safe, yet he meant, far more than that, being kept true.

When John Love called at Johnson's cottage to fetch Robert Purcas, the two walked about a hundred yards on the way to Bentley without either speaking a word. Then Robert suddenly stopped. "Look you, Love! what would you with me? I cannot go far from Thorpe to-night. I was sent with a message to Johnson, and I have not found a chance to deliver it yet."

"Must it be to-night? and what chance look you for?"

"Ay, it must!" answered Robert earnestly. "What I look for is yon black snake coming out of his hole, and then slip I in and deliver my message."

Love nodded. He knew well enough who the black snake was. "Then maybe you came with the like word I did. Was it to warn Johnson to 'scape ere the Bailiff should be on him?"

"Ay, it was. And you?"

"I came to the same end, but not alone for Johnson. Robin, thou hadst best see to thyself. Dost know thou art on the black list.

"I've looked for that, this many a day. But so art thou, Love; and thou hast a wife to care for, and I've none."

"I'm in danger anyway, Rob, but there's a chance for thee. Think of thy old father, and haste thee, lad."

Robert shook his head. "I promised to warn Johnson," he said; "and I gave my word for it to one that I love right dearly. I'll not break my word. No, Love; I tarry here till I've seen him. The Lord must have a care of my old father if they take me."

Love found it impossible to move Robert from his resolution. He bade him good-night and turned away.

CHAPTER XVIII.

WHAT BEFELL SOME OF THEM.

OR half-an-hour, safely hidden behind a hedge, Robert Purcas watched the door of Johnson's cottage, until at last he saw the priest come out, and go up the lane for a short distance. Then he stopped, looked round, and gave a low, peculiar whistle. A man jumped down from the bank on the other side of the lane, with whom the priest held a long, low-toned conversation. Robert knew he could not safely move before they were out of the way. At length they parted, and he just caught the priest's final words.

"Good: we shall have them all afore the even."

"That you shall not, if God speed me!" said Robert to himself.

The priest went up the lane towards Bentley, and the man who had been talking with him took the opposite way to Thorpe. When his footsteps had died away, Robert crept out from the shelter of the hedge, and made his way in the dark to Johnson's cottage. A rap on the door brought Cissy.

"Who is it, please?" she said, "because I can't see."

"It is Robin Purcas, Cis. I want a word with thy father."

"Come in, Robin!" called Johnson's voice from within. "I could see thou wert bursting with some news

not to be spoken in the presence but just gone. What
ails thee, man?"

"Ay, I was, and I promised to tell you. Jack, thou
must win away ere daylight, or the Bailiff shall be on
thee. Set these little ones in safe guard, and hie thee
away with all the speed thou mayest."

"Is it come so near?" said Johnson, gravely.

"Father, you're not going nowhere without me!"
said Cissy, creeping up to him, and slipping her hand
in his. "You can leave Will and Baby with Neighbour
Ursula: but I'll not be left unless you bid me—and you
won't Father? You can never do without me? I must
go where you go."

"She's safe, I reckon," said Robert, answering Johnson's look: "they'd never do no mischief to much as
she. Only maybe she'd be more out of reach if I took
her with me. They'll seek to breed her up in a convent, most like."

Cissy felt her father's hand tighten upon hers.

"I'm not going with you, nor nobody!" said she.
"I'll go with Father. Nobody'll get me nowhere else,
without they carry me."

Johnson seemed to wake up, as if till then he had
scarcely understood what it all meant.

"God bless thee for the warning, lad!" he said.
"Now hie thee quick, and get out of reach thyself
Cis, go up and fetch a warm wrap for Baby, and all her
clothes; I'll take her next door. I reckon Will must
tarry there too. It'd be better for thee, Cis: but I'll
not compel thee, if thy little heart's set on going with
me. Thoul't have to rough it, little maid."

"I'll not stop nowhere!" was Cissy's determination.

Robert bade them good-bye with a smile, closed the
door, and set off down the lane as fast as the darkness
made it prudent. He did not think it wise to go through

the village, so he made a *détour* by some fields, and came
into the road again on the other side of Thorpe. He
had not gone many yards, when he became aware that
a number of lights were approaching, accompanied by
a noise of voices. Robert turned straight round. If
he could get back to the stile which led into the fields,
he would be safer: and if not, still it would be better
to be overtaken than to meet a possible enemy face to
face. He would be less likely to be noticed in the
former case than in the latter—at least so he thought.

There must be a good number of people coming behind him, judging from the voices. At length they
came up with him.

"Pray you, young man, how far be we from Thorpe?"

"You are very nigh, straight on," was Robert's
answer.

"Do you belong there?"

"No, I'm nigh a stranger to these parts: I'm from
the eastern side of the county. I can't tell you much
about folks, if that be your meaning."

"And what do you here, if you be a stranger?"

"I've a job o' work at St. Osyth, at this present."

"What manner of work?"

"I'm a fuller by trade."

Robert had already recognised that he was talking to
the Bailiff's searching party. Every minute that he
could keep them was a minute more for Johnson and
the little ones.

"Know you a man named Johnson?"

"What, here?"

"Ay, at Thorpe."

Robert pretended to consider. "Well, let's see—
there's Will Johnson the miller, and Luke Johnson the
weaver, and—eh, there's ever so many Johnsons! I
couldn't say to one or another, without I knew more."

" John Johnson ; he's a labouring man."

" Well, there is Johnsons that lives up by the wood, but I'm none so sure of the man's name. I think it's Andrew, but I'll not say, certain. It may be John; I couldn't speak, not to be sure."

" Let him be, Gregory ; he knows nought," said the Bailiff.

Robert touched his cap, and fell behind. The Bailiff suddenly turned round.

" What's your own name ? "

It was a terrible temptation! If he gave a false name, the strong probability was that they would pass on, and he would very likely get safe away. It was Johnson of whom they were thinking, not himself. But that would enable them to reach Johnson's cottage a minute sooner, and it would be a cowardly lie. No! Robert Purcas had not so learned Christ. He gave his name honestly.

" Robert Purcas! If that's not on my list——" said the Bailiff, feeling in his pocket. " Ay, here it is—stay! *William* Purcas, of Bocking, fuller, aged twenty, single ; is that you ? "

" My name is Robert, not William," said the young man.

" But thou art a fuller ? and single? and aged twenty ? "

" Ay, all that is so."

" Dost thou believe the bread of the sacred host to be transmuted after consecration into the body of Christ, so that no substance of bread is left there at all ? "

" I do not. I cannot, for I see the bread."

" He's a heretic ! " cried Simnel. " Robert or William, it is all one. Take the heretic ! "

And so Robert Purcas was seized, and carried to the Moot Hall in Colchester—a fate from which one word of falsehood would have freed him, but it would have cost him his Father's smile.

The Moot Hall of Colchester was probably the oldest municipal building in England. It was erected soon after the Conquest, and its low circular arches and piers ornamented the High Street until 1843, when the town Vandals were pleased to destroy it because it impeded the traffic. Robert was taken into the dungeon, and the great door slammed to behind him. He could not see for a few minutes, coming fresh from the light of day: and before he was able to make anything out clearly, an old lady's voice accosted him.

"Robert Purcas, if I err not?" she said. "I am sorry to behold thee here, friend."

"Truly, Mistress, more than I am, that am come hither in Christ's cause."

"Ay? Then thou art well come."

"Methinks it is Mistress Silverside?"

"Thou sayest well. I shall have company now," said the old lady with a smile. "Methought some of my brethren and sisters should be like to have after."

"I reckon," responded Purcas, "we be sure at the least of our Father's company."

The great door just then rolled back, and they heard the gaoler's voice outside.

"Gramercy, but this is tidy work!" cried he. "Never had no such prisoners here afore. I don't know what to do with 'em. There, get you in! you aren't the first there."

There was a moment's pause, and then Mrs. Silverside and Robert, who were looking to see what uncommon sort of prisoners could be at hand, found that their eyes had to come down considerably nearer the floor, as the gaoler let in, hand in hand, Cissy and Will Johnson, followed by their father.

CHAPTER XIX

"*FATHER'S COME TOO!*"

HY, my dear hearts!" cried old Mrs. Silverside, as the children came in. "How won ye hither?"

"Please, we haven't been naughty," said Will, rubbing his eyes with his knuckles.

"Father's come too, so it's all right," added Cissy in a satisfied tone.

Mrs. Silverside turned to Robert Purcas. "Is not here a lesson for thee and me, my brother? Our Father is come too: God is with us, and thus it is all right."

"Marry, these heretics beareth a good brag!" said Wastborowe the gaoler to his man.

It is bad grammar now to use a singular verb with a plural noun; but in 1556 it was correct English over the whole south of England, and the use of the singular with the singular, or the plural with the plural, was a peculiarity of the northern dialect.

"They always doth," answered the under-gaoler.

"Will ye be of as good courage, think you," asked Wastborowe, "the day ye stand up by Colne Water?"

"God knoweth," was the reverent answer of Mrs. Silverside. "If He holds us up, then shall we stand."

"They be safe kept whom He keepeth," said Johnson.

"Please, Mr. Wastborowe," said Cissy in a business-

like manner, "would you mind telling me when we shall
be burned ? "

The gaoler turned round and stared at his questioner.

"Thou aren't like to be burned, I reckon," said he
with a laugh.

"I must, if Father is," was Cissy's calm response.
"It'll hurt a bit, I suppose ; but you see when we get
to Heaven afterwards, every thing will be so good and
pleasant, I don't think we need care much. Do you,
please, Mr. Wastborowe ? "

"Marry come up, thou scrap of a chirping canary ! "
answered the gaoler, half roughly and half amused.
"If babes like this be in such minds, 'tis no marvel their
fathers and mothers stand to it."

"But I'm not a baby, Mr. Wastborowe ! " said Cissy,
rather affronted. "Will and Baby are both younger than
me. I'm going in ten, and I takes care of Father."

Mr. Wastborowe, who was drinking ale out of a huge
tankard, removed it from his lips to laugh.

"Mighty good care thou'lt take, I'll be bound ! "

"Yes, I do, Mr. Wastborowe," replied Cissy, quite
gravely ; "I dress Father's meat and mend his clothes,
and love him. That's taking care of him, isn't it ? "

The gaoler's men, who were accustomed to see every
body in the prison appear afraid of him, were evidently
much amused by the perfect fearlessness of Cissy.
Wastborowe himself seemed to think it a very good joke.

"And who takes care of thee ? " asked he.

Cissy gave her usual answer. "God takes care of me."

"And not of thy father ? " said Wastborowe with a
sneer.

The sneer passed by Cissy quite harmlessly.

"God takes care of all of us," she said. "He helps
Father to take care of me, and He helps me to take
care of Father."

"He'll bo taken goodly care of whon he's burned," said the gaoler coarsely, taking another draught out of the tankard.

Cissy considered that point.

"Please, Mr. Wastborowe, we mustn't expect to be taken better care of than the Lord Jesus; and He had to suffer, you know. But it won't signify when we get to Heaven, I suppose."

"Heretics don't go to Heaven!" replied Wastborowe.

"I don't know what heretics are," said Cissy; "but every body who loves the Lord Jesus is sure to get there. Satan would not want them, you know; and Jesus will want them, for He died for them. He'll look after us, I expect. Don't you think so, Mr. Wastborowe?"

"Hold thy noise!" said the gaoler, rising, with the empty jug in his hand. He wanted some more ale, and he was tired of amusing himself with Cissy.

"Hush thee, my little maid!" said her father, laying his hand on her head.

"Is he angry, Father?" asked Cissy, looking up. "I said nothing wrong, did I?"

"There's somewhat wrong," responded he, "but it's not thee, child."

Meanwhile Wastborowe was crossing the court to his own house, jug in hand. Opening the door, he set down the jug on the table, with the short command, "Fill that."

"You may tarry till I've done," answered Audrey, calmly ironing on. She was the only person in the place who was not afraid of her husband. In fact, he was afraid of her when, as he expressed it, she "was wrong side up."

"Come, wife! I can't wait," replied Wastborowe in a tone which he never used to any living creature but Audrey or a priest.

Audrey coolly set down the iron on its stand, folded

up the shirt which she had just finished, and laid another
on the board.

"You can. wait uncommon well, John Wastborowe,"
said she; "you've had as much as is good for you already, and maybe a bit to spare. I can't leave my
ironing."

"Am I to get it myself, then?" asked the gaoler,
sulkily.

"Just as you please," was the calm response. "I'm
not going."

Wastborowe took up his jug, went to the cellar, and
drew the ale for himself, in a meek, subdued style, very
different indeed from the aspect which he wore to his
prisoners. He had scarcely left the door when a shrill
voice summoned him to—

"Come back and shut the door, thou blundering
dizzard! When will men ever have a bit of sense?"

The gaoler came back to shut the door, and then,
returning to the dungeon, showed himself so excessively
surly and overbearing, that his men whispered to one
another that "he'd been having it out with his mistress." Before he recovered his equanimity, the Bailiff
returned and called him into the courtyard.

"Hearken, Wastborowe: how many of these have
you now in ward? Well-nigh all, methinks." And he
read over the list. "Elizabeth Wood, Christian Hare,
Rose Fletcher, Joan Kent, Agnes Stanley, Margaret
Simson, Robert Purcas, Agnes Silverside, John Johnson,
Elizabeth Foulkes."

"Got 'em all save that last," said Wastborowe.

"Who is she? I know not the name. By the same
token, what didst with the babe? There were three of
Johnson's children, and one in arms."

"Left it wi' Jane Hiltoft," said the gaoler, gruffly.
"I didn't want it screeching here."

The Bailiff nodded. "Maybe she can tell us who this woman is," said he; and stepping a little nearer the porter's lodge, he summoned the porter's wife.

Mrs. Hiltoft came to the door with little Helen Johnson in her arms. "Well, I don't know," said she. "I'll tell you what: you'd best ask Audrey Wastborowe; she's a bit of a gossip, and I reckon she knows everybody in Colchester, by name and face, if no more. She'll tell you if anybody can."

The Bailiff stepped across the court, and rapped at the gaoler's door. He was desired by a rather shrill voice to come in. He just opened the door about an inch, and spoke through it.

"Audrey, do you know aught of one Elizabeth Foulkes?"

"Liz'beth What-did-you-say?" inquired Mrs. Wastborowe, hastily drying her arms on her apron, and coming forward.

"Elizabeth Foulkes," repeated the Bailiff.

"What, yon lass o' Clere's the clothier? Oh, ay, you'll find her in Balcon Lane, at the Magpie. A tall, well-favoured young maid she is—might be a princess, to look at her. What's she been doing, now?"

"Heresy," said the Bailiff, shortly.

"Heresy! dear, dear, to think of it! Well, now, who could have thought it? But Master Clere's a bit unsteady in that way, his self, ain't he?"

"Oh nay, he's reconciled."

"Oh!" The tone was significant.

"Why, was you wanting yon maid o' Mistress Clere's?" said the porter's wife. "You'll have her safe enough, for I met Amy Clere this even, and she said her mother was downright vexed with their Bess, and had turned the key on her. I did not know it was her you meant. I've never heard her called nought but Bess, you see."

"Then that's all well," said Maynard. "I'll tarry for her till the morrow, for I'm well wearied to-night."

CHAPTER XX

LED TO THE SLAUGHTER.

HE long hours of that day wore on, and nobody came again to Elizabeth in the porch-chamber. The dusk fell, and she heard the sounds of locking up the house and going to bed, and began to understand that neither supper nor bed awaited her that night. Elizabeth quietly cleared a space on the floor in the moonlight, heaping boxes and baskets on one another, till she had room to lie down, and then, after kneeling to pray, she slept more peacefully than Queen Mary did in her Palace. She was awoke suddenly at last. It was broad daylight, and somebody was rapping at the street door.

"Amy!" she heard Mistress Clere call from her bed-chamber, "look out and see who is there."

Amy slept at the front of the house, in the room next to the porch-chamber. Elizabeth rose to her feet, giving her garments a shake down as the only form of dressing just then in her power, and looked out of the window.

The moment she did so she knew that one of the supreme moments of her life had come. Before the door stood Mr. Maynard, the Bailiff of Colchester—the man who had marched off the twenty-three prisoners to London in the previous August. Everybody who knew him knew that he was a "stout Papist," to whom it was dear delight to bring a Protestant to punishment. Elizabeth did not doubt for an instant that she was the one chosen for his next victim.

Just as Amy Clere put her head out of the window. Mr. Maynard, who did not reckon patience among his chief virtues, and who was tired of waiting, signed to one of his men to give another sharp rap, accompanied by a shout of—"Open, in the Queen's name!"

"Saints, love us and help us!" ejaculated Amy, taking her head in again. "Mother, it's the Queen's men!"

"Go down and open to 'em," was Mrs. Clere's next order.

"Eh, I durstn't if it was ever so!" screamed Amy in reply. "May I unlock the door and send Bessy?"

"Thee do as thou art bid!" came in the gruff tones of her father.

"Come, I'll go with thee," said her mother. "Tell Master Bailiff we're at hand, or they'll mayhap break the door in."

A third violent rap enforced Mrs. Clere's command.

"Have a bit of patience, Master Bailiff!" cried Amy from her window. "We're a-coming as quick as may be. Let a body get some clothes on, do!"

Somebody under the window was heard to laugh.

Then Mrs. Clere went downstairs, her heavy tread followed by the light run of her daughter's steps; and then Elizabeth heard the bolts drawn back, and the Bailiff and his men march into the kitchen of the Magpie.

"Good-morrow, Mistress Clere. I am verily sorry to come to the house of a good Catholic on so ill an errand. But I am in search of a maid of yours, by name Elizabeth Foulkes, whose name hath been presented afore the Queen's Grace's Commission for heresy. Is this the maid ? "

Mr. Maynard, as he spoke, laid his hand not very gently on Amy's shoulder.

"Eh, bless me, no ! " cried **Amy**, in terror. " I'm as good a Catholic as you or any. I'll say aught you want me, and I don't care what it is—that the moon's made o' green cheese, if you will, and I'd a shive last night for supper. Don't take *me*, for mercy's sake ! "

" I'm not like," said Mr. Maynard, laughing, and giving Amy a rough pat on the back. " You aren't the sort I want."

" You're after Bess Foulkes, aren't you ? " said Mrs. Clere. " Amy, there's the key. Go fetch her down. I locked her up, you see, that she should be safe when wanted. I'm a true woman to Queen and Church, I am, Master Bailiff. You'll find no heresy here, outside yon jade of a Bessy."

Mrs. Clere knew well that suspicion had attached to her husband's name in time past, which made her more desirous to free herself from all complicity with what the authorities were pleased to call heresy.

Amy ran upstairs and unlocked the door of the porch-chamber.

" Bessy, the Bailiff's come for thee ! "

A faint flush rose to Elizabeth's face as she stood up.

" Now do be discreet, Bessy, and say as he says. Bless you, it's only words ! I told him I'd say the moon was made o' green cheese if he wanted. Why shouldn't you ? "

" Mistress Amy, it would be dishonour to my Lord, and I am ready for anything but that."

" Good lack ! couldst not do a bit o' penance at after? Bess, it's thy life that's in danger. Do be wise in time, lass."

"It is only this life," said Elizabeth quietly, "and 'he that saveth his life shall lose it.' They that be faithful to the end shall have the crown of life.—Master Bailiff, I am ready."

The Bailiff looked up at the fair, tall, queenly maiden who stood before him.

"I trust thou art ready to submit to the Church," he said. "It were sore pity thou shouldst lose life and all things."

"Nay, I desire to win them," answered Elizabeth. "I am right ready to submit to all which it were good for me to submit to."

"Come, well said!" replied the Bailiff; and he tied the cord round her hands, and led her away to the Moot Hall.

Just stop and think a moment, what it would be to be led in this way through the streets of a town where nearly everybody knew you, as if you had been a thief or a murderer!—led by a cord like an animal about to be sold—nay, as our Master, Christ, was led, like a sheep to the slaughter! Fancy what it would be, to a girl who had always been respectable and well-behaved to be used in this way: to hear the rough, coarse jokes of the bystanders and of the men who were leading her, and not to have one friend with her—not one living creature that cared what became of her, except that Lord who had once died for her, and for whom she was now, for aught she knew, upon her way to die! And even He *seemed* as if He did not care. Men did these things, and He kept silence. Don't you think it was hard to bear?

When Elizabeth reached the Moot Hall and was taken to the prison, for an instant she felt as if she had reached home and friends. Mrs. Silverside bade her welcome with a kindly smile, and Robert Purcas came up and kissed her—people kissed each other then instead of shaking hands as we do now,—and Elizabeth felt their sympathy a true comfort. But she was calm under her suffering until she caught sight of Cissy. Then an exclamation of pain broke from her.

"O Cissy, Cissy; I am so sorry for thee!"

"O Bessy, but I'm so glad! Don't say you're sorry."

"Why, Cissy, how canst thou be glad? Dost know what it all signifieth?"

"I know they've taken Father, and I'm sorry enough for that; but then Father always said they would some day. But don't you see why I'm glad? They've got me too. I was always proper 'feared they'd take Father and leave me all alone with the children; and he'd have missed us dreadful! Now, you see, I can tend on him, and do everything for him; and that's why I'm glad. If it had to be, you know."

Elizabeth looked up at Cissy's father, and he said in a husky voice,—

"'Of such is the kingdom of Heaven.'"

CHAPTER XXI

BEFORE THE COMMISSIONERS.

ESSY," said Cissy in a whisper, "do you think they'll burn us all to-day?"

"I reckon, sweet heart, they be scarce like to burn thee."

"But they'll have to do to me whatever they do to Father!" cried Cissy, earnestly.

"Dear child, thou wist not what burning is."

"Oh, but I've burnt my fingers before now," said Cissy, with an air of extensive experience which would have suited an old woman. "It's not proper pleasant: but the worst's afterwards, and there wouldn't be any afterwards, would there? It would be Heaven after·wards, wouldn't it? I don't see that there's so much to be 'feared of in being burnt. If they didn't burn me, and did Will and Baby, and—and Father"—and Cissy's voice faltered, and she began to sob—"that would be dreadful—dreadful! O Bessy, won't you ask God not to give them leave? They couldn't, could they, unless He did?"

"Nay, dear heart, not unless He did," answered Elizabeth, feeling her own courage strengthened by the child's faith.

"Then if you and I both ask Him *very* hard,—O Bessy! don't you think He will?"

Before Elizabeth could answer, Johnson said,—"I wouldn't, Cis."

"You wouldn't, Father! Please why?"

"Because, dear heart, He knoweth better than we what is good for us. Sometimes, when folk ask God too earnestly for that they desire, He lets them have it, but in punishment, not in mercy. It would have been a sight better for the Israelites if they hadn't had those quails. Dost thou mind how David saith, 'He gave them their desire, but sent leanness withall into their souls?' I'd rather be burnt, Cis, than live with a lean soul, and my Father in Heaven turning away His face from me."

Cissy considered. "Father, I could never get along a bit, if you were so angry you wouldn't look at me!"

"Truly, dear heart, and I would not have my Father so. Ask the Lord what thou wilt, Cis, if it be His will; only remember that His will is best for us—the happiest as well as the most profitable."

"Wilt shut up o' thy preachment?" shouted Wastborowe, with a severe blow to Johnson. "Thou wilt make the child as ill an heretic as thyself, and we mean to bring her up a good Catholic Christian!"

Johnson made no answer to the gaoler's insolent command. A look of great pain came into his face, and he lifted his head up towards the sky, as if he were holding communion with his Father in Heaven. Elizabeth guessed his thoughts. If he were to be martyred, and his little helpless children to be handed over to the keeping of priests who would teach them to commit idolatry, and forbid them to read the Bible— that seemed a far worse prospect in his eyes than even the agony of seeing them suffer. That, at the worst, would be an hour's anguish, to be followed by an eternity of happy rest: but the other might mean the loss of all things—body and soul alike. Little Will did not enter into the matter. He might have understood something if he had been paying attention, but he was not attending, and therefore he did not. But Cissy, to whom her father was the centre of the world, and who knew his voice by heart, understood his looks as readily as his words.

"Father!" she said, looking at him, "don't be troubled about us. I'll never believe nobody that says different from what you've learned us, and I'll tell Will and Baby they mustn't mind them neither."

And Elizabeth added softly—"'I will be a God to thee, and to thy seed after thee.' 'Leave thy fatherless children; I will preserve them alive.'"

"God bless you both!" said Johnson. and he could say no more.

The next day the twelve prisoners accused of heresy were had up for examination before the Commissioners, Sir John Kingston, Mr. Roper, and Mr. Boswell, the Bishop's scribe. Six of them—Elizabeth Wood, Christian Hare, Rose Fletcher, Joan Kent, Agnes Stanley, and Margaret Simson—were soon disposed of. They had been in prison for a fortnight or more, they were terribly frightened, and they were not strong in the faith. They easily consented to be reconciled to the Church—to say whatever the priests bade them, and to believe—or pretend to believe—all that they were desired.

Robert Purcas was the next put on trial. The Bishop's scribe called him (in the account he wrote to his master) "obstinate, and a glorious prating heretic." What this really meant was that his arguments were too powerful to answer. He must have had considerable ability, for though only twenty years of age, and a village tradesman, he was set down in the charge-sheet as "lettered," namely, a well-educated man, which in those days was most extraordinary for a man of that description.

" When confessed you last ? " asked the Commissioners of Purcas.

" I have not confessed of long time," was the answer, " nor will I; for priests have no power to remit sin."

" Come you to church, to hear the holy mass ? "

" I do not, nor will I; for all that is idolatry."

" Have you never, then, received the blessed Sacrament of the altar ? "

" I did receive the Supper of the Lord in King Edward's time, but not since : nor will I, except it be ministered to me as it was then."

" Do you not worship the sacred host ? "

That is, the consecrated bread in the Lord's Supper.

" Those who worship it are idolators ! " said Robert Purcas, without the least hesitation : " that which there is used is bread and wine only."

" Have him away ! " cried Sir John Kingston. " What need to question further so obstinate a man ? "

So they had him away—not being able to answer him —and Agnes Silverside was called in his stead.

She was very calm, but as determined as Purcas.

" Come hither, Mistress ! " said Boswell, roughly. " Why, what have we here in the charge-sheet ? ' Agnes Silverside, *alias* Smith, *alias* Downes, *alias* May !' Hast thou had four husbands, old witch, or how comest by so many names ? "

" Sir," was the quiet answer, " my name is Smith from my father, and I have been thrice wed."

The Commissioners, having first amused themselves by a little rough joking at the prisoner's expense, inquired which of her husbands was the last.

" My present name is Silverside," she replied.

" And what was he, this Silverside ?—a tanner or a chimney-sweep ? "

" Sir, he was a priest."

The Commissioners—who knew it all beforehand— professed themselves exceedingly shocked. God never forbade priests to marry under the Old Testament, nor did He ever command Christian ministers to be unmarried men: but the Church of Rome has forbidden her priests to have any wives, as St. Paul told Timothy would be done by those who departed from the faith: * thus "teaching for doctrines the commandments of men." †

* 1 Tim. iv. 3.   † Matt. xv. 9.

CHAPTER XXII

GENTLY HANDLED.

HEN the Commissioners had tormented the priest's widow as long as they thought proper, they called on her to answer the charges brought against her.

"Dost thou believe that in the blessed Sacrament of the altar the bread and wine becometh the very body and blood of Christ, so soon as the word of consecration be pronounced?"

"Nay: it is but bread and wine before it is received; and when it is received in faith and ministered by a worthy minister, then it is Christ flesh and blood spiritually, and not otherwise."

"Dost though worship the blessed Sacrament?"

"Truly, nay: for ye make the Sacrament an idol. It ought not to be worshipped with knocking, kneeling or holding up of hands."

"Wilt thou come to church and hear mass?"

"That will I not, so long as ye do worship to other than God Almighty. Nothing that is made can be the same thing as he that made it. They must needs be idolators, and of the meanest sort, that worship the works of their own hands."

"Aroint thee, old witch! Wilt thou go to confession?"

"Neither will I that, for no priest hath power to remit sin that is against God. To Him surely will I confess: and having so done, I have no need to make confession to men."

"Take the witch away!" cried the chief Commissioner. ".She's a froward, obstinate heretic, only fit to make firewood."

The gaoler led her out of the court, and John Johnson was summoned next.

"What is thy name, and how old art thou?"

"My name is John Johnson; I am a labouring man, of the age of four and thirty years."

"Canst read?"

"But a little."

"Then how darest thou set thee up against the holy doctors of the Church, that can read Latin?"

"Cannot a man be saved without he read Latin?"

"Hold thine impudent tongue! It is our business to question, and thine to answer. Where didst learn thy pestilent doctrine?"

"I learned the Gospel of Christ Jesus, if that be what you mean by pestilent doctrine, from Master Trudgeon at the first. He learned me that the Sacrament, as ye minister it, is an idol, and that no priest hath power to remit sin."

"Dost thou account of this Trudgeon as a true prophet?"

"Ay, I do."

"What then sayest thou to our Saviour Christ's word to His Apostles, 'Whosesoever sins ye remit, they are remitted unto them'?"

"Marry, I say nought, without you desire it."

"What meanest by that?"

"Why, you are not apostles, nor yet the priests that be now alive. He said not, 'Whosesoever sins Sir Thomas Tye shall remit, they are remitted unto them.'"

"Thou foolish man, Sir Thomas Tye is successor of the apostles."

"Well, but it sayeth not neither, 'Whosesoever sins ye and your successors do remit.' I'll take the words as they stand, by your leave. To apostles were they said, and to apostles will I leave them."

"The man hath no reason in him!" said Kingston. "Have him away likewise."

"Please your Worships," said the gaoler, "here be all that are indicted. There is but one left, and she was presented only for not attending at mass nor confession."

"Bring her up!"

And Elizabeth Foulkes stepped up to the table, and courtesied to the representatives of the Queen.

"What is thy name?"

"Elizabeth Foulkes."

"How old art thou?"

"Twenty years."

"Art thou a wife?"

Girls commonly married then younger than they do now. The usual length of human life was shorter: people who reached sixty were looked upon as we now regard those of eighty, and a man of seventy was considered much as one of ninety or more would be at the present time.

"Nay, I am a maid," said Elizabeth.

The word maid was only just beginning to be used instead of servant; it generally meant an unmarried woman.

"What is thy calling?"

"I am servant to Master Nicholas Clere, clothier, of Balcon Lane."

"Art Colchester-born?"

"I was born at Stoke Nayland, in Suffolk."

"And wherefore dost thou not come to mass?"

"Because I hold the Sacrament of the altar to be

but bread and wine, which may not be worshipped under peril of idolatry."

"Well, and why comest not to confession?"

"Because no priest hath power to remit sins."

"Hang 'em! they are all in a story!" said the chief Commissioner, wrathfully. "But she's a well-favoured maid, this: it were verily pity to burn her, if we could win her to recant."

What a poor, weak, mean thing human nature is! The men who had no pity for the white hair of Agnes Silverside, or the calm courage of John Johnson, or even the helpless innocence of little Cissy: such things as these did not touch them at all—these very men were anxious to save Elizabeth Foulkes, not because she was good, but because she was beautiful.

It is a sad, sad blunder, which people often make, to set beauty above goodness. Some very wicked things have been done in this world, simply by thinking too much of beauty. Admiration is a good thing in its proper place; but a great deal of mischief comes when it gets into the wrong one. Whenever you admire a bad man because he is clever, or a foolish woman because she is pretty, you are letting admiration get out of his place. If we had lived when the Lord Jesus was upon earth, we should not have found people admiring Him. He was not beautiful. "His face was marred more than any man, and His form more than the sons of men." And would it not have been dreadful if we had admired Pontius Pilate and Judas Iscariot, and had seen no beauty in Him who is "altogether lovely" to the hearts of those whom the Holy Ghost has taught to love Him? So take care what sort of beauty you admire, and make sure that goodness goes along with it. We may be quite certain that however much men thought of Elizabeth's beautiful face, God thought very little of it. The beauty

which He saw in her was her love to the Lord Jesus,
and her firm stand against what would dishonour Him.
This sort of beauty all of us can have. Oh, do ask God
to make you beautiful in *His* eyes!

No sooner had the chief Commissioner spoken than a
voice in the Court called out,—

"Pray you, Worshipful Sirs, save this young maid!
I am her mother's brother, Thomas Holt of Colchester,
and I do you to wit she is of a right good inclination,
and no wise perverse. I do entreat you, grant her yet
another chance."

Then a gentleman stepped forward from the crowd of
listeners.

"Worshipful Sirs," said he, "may I have leave to
take charge of this young maiden, to the end that she
may be reconciled to the Church, and obtain remission
of her errors? Truly, as Master Commissioner saith,
it were pity so fair a creature were made food for the
fire."

"Who are you?—and what surety give you?" asked
Sir John.

Sir Thomas Tye rose from his seat on the Bench.

"Please it, your Worships, that is Master Ashby of
this town, a good Catholic man, and well to be trusted.
If your Worships be pleased to show mercy to the maid,
as indeed I would humbly entreat you to do, there were
no better man than he to serve you in this matter."

The priest having spoken in favour of Mr. Ashby the
Commissioners required no further surety.

"Art thou willing to be reformed?" they asked
Elizabeth.

"Sirs," she answered cautiously, "I am willing to be
shown God's true way, if so be I err from it."

This was enough for the Commissioners. They wanted
to set her free, and they therefore accepted from her

words which would probably have been used in vain by the rest. Mr. Ashby was charged to keep and "reconcile" her, which he promised to do, or to feed her on barley bread if she proved obstinate.

As Elizabeth turued to follow him she passed close by Robert Purcas, whom the gaoler was just about to take back to prison.

" 'Thou hast set them in slippery places,' " whispered Purcas as she passed him. " Keep thou true to Christ. O Elizabeth, mine own love, keep true ! "

The tears rose to Elizabeth's eyes. " Pray ror me, Robin," she said. And then each was led away.

CHAPTER XXIII.

RESPITE.

THE Commissioners who tried these prisoners were thoroughly worldly men, who really cared nothing about the doctrines which they burned people for not believing. Had it been otherwise, when Queen Elizabeth came to the throne, less than two years afterwards, these men would have shown themselves willing to suffer in their turn. But most of them did not do this—seldom even to the extent of losing promotion, scarcely ever to that of losing life. They simply wheeled round again to what they had been in the reign of Edward VI.

It is possible to respect men who are willing to lose their lives for the sake of what they believe to be true, even though you may think them quite mistaken. But how can you respect a man who will not run the risk of losing a situation or a few pounds in defence of the truth? It is not possible.

After the trial of the Colchester prisoners, the Commissioners passed on to other places, and the town was quiet for a time. Mrs. Silverside, Johnson and the children, and Purcas, remained in prison in the Moot Hall, and Elizabeth Foulkes was as truly a prisoner in the house of Henry Ashby. At first she was very kindly treated, in the hope of inducing her to recant.

But as time went on, things were altered. Mr. Ashby found that what Elizabeth understood by "being shown God's true way," was not being argued with by a priest, nor being commanded to obey the Church, but being pointed to some passage in the Bible which agreed with what he said; and since what he said was not in accordance with the Bible, of course he could not show her any texts which agreed with it.

The Church of Rome herself admits that people who read the Bible for themselves generally become Protestants. Does not common sense show that in that case the Protestant doctrines must be the doctrines of the Bible? Why should Rome be so anxious to shut up the Bible if her own doctrines are to be found there?

Above four months passed on, and no change came to the prisoners, but there had not been any fresh arrests. The other Gospellers began to breathe more freely, and to hope that the worst had come already. Mrs. Wade was left at liberty; Mr. Ewring had not been taken; surely all would go well now!

How often we think the worst must be over, just a minute before it comes upon us!

A little rap on Margaret Thurston's door brought her to open it.

"Why, Rose! I'm fain to see thee, maid. Come in."

"My mother bade me tell you, Margaret," said Rose, when the door was shut, "that there shall be a Scripture reading in our house this even. Will you come?"

"That will we, right gladly, dear heart. At what hour?"

"Midnight. We dare not afore."

"We'll be there. How fares thy mother to-day?"

"Why, not over well. She seems but ill at ease. Her hands burn, and she is ever athirst. 'Tis an ill rheum, methinks."

I

"Aye, she has caught a bad cold," said Margaret. "Rose, I'll tell you what—we'll come a bit afore midnight, and see if we cannot help you. My master knows a deal touching herbs; he's well-nigh as good as any apothecary, though I say it, and he'll compound an herb drink that shall do her good, with God's blessing, while I help you in the house. What say you? Have I well said?"

"Indeed, Margaret, and I'd be right thankful if you would, for it'll be hard on Father if he's neither Mother nor me to do for him—she, sick abed, and me waiting on her."

"Be sure it will! But I hope it'll not be so bad as that. Well, then, look you, we'll shut up the hut and come after you. You haste on to her, and when I've got things a bit tidy, and my master's come from work —he looked to be overtime to-night—we'll run over to Bentley, and do what we can."

Rose thanked her again, and went on with increased speed. She found her mother no better, and urged her to go to bed, telling her that Margaret was close at hand. It was now about five in the afternoon.

Alice agreed to this, for she felt almost too poorly to sit up. She went to bed, and Rose flew about the kitchen, getting all finished that she could before Margaret should arrive.

It was Saturday night, and the earliest hours of the Sabbath were to be ushered in by the "reading." Only a few neighbours were asked, for it was necessary now to be very careful. Half-a-dozen might be invited, as if to supper; but the times when a hundred or more had assembled to hear the Word of God were gone by. Would they ever come again? They dared not begin to read until all prying eyes and ears were likely to be closed in sleep; and the reader's voice was low, that nobody might be roused next door. Few people could read then, especially among the labouring class, so that, except on these occasions, the poorer Gospellers had no hope of hearing the words of the Lord.

The reading was over, and one after another of the guests stole silently out into the night—black, noiseless shadows, going up the lane into the village, or down it on the way to Thorpe. At length the last was gone except the Thurstons, who offered to stay for the night. John Thurston lay down in the kitchen, and Margaret, finding Alice Mount apparently better, said she would share Rose's bed.

Alice Mount's malady was what we call a bad feverish cold, and generally we do not expect it to do anything more than make the patient very uncomfortable for a week. But in Queen Mary's days they knew very much less about colds than we do, and they were much more afraid of them. It was only six years since the last attack of the terrible sweating sickness—the last ever to be, but they did not know that—and people were always frightened of anything like a cold turning to that dreadful epidemic wherein, as King Edward VI. writes in his diary, "if one took cold he died within three hours, and if he escaped, it held him but nine hours, or ten at the most." It was, therefore, a relief to hear Alice say that she felt better, and urge Rose to go to bed.

"Well, it scarce seems worth while going to bed," said Margaret. "What time is it? Can you see the church clock, Rose?"

"We can when it's light," said Rose; "but I think you'll not see it now."

Margaret drew back the little curtain, but all was dark, and she let it drop again.

"It'll be past one, I reckon," said she.

"Oh, ay; a good way on toward two," was Rose's answer.

"Rose, have you heard aught of Bessy Foulkes of late ?"

"Nought. I've tried to see her, but they keep her so close at Master Ashby's there's no getting to her."

"And those poor little children of Johnson's They're yet in prison, trow ?"

"Oh, ay. I wish they'd have let us have the baby Jane Hiltoft has it. She'll care it well enough for the body : but for the soul——"

"Oh, when Johnson's burned—as he will be, I reckon —the children'll be bred up in convents, be sure," was Margaret's answer.

"Nay! I'll be sure of nought so bad as that, as long as God's in heaven."

"There's no miracles now o' days, Rose."

"There's God's care, just as much as in Elijah's days. And, Margaret, they've burned little children afore now."

"Eh, don't, Rose! you give me the cold chills!"

"What's that ?" Rose was listening intently.

"What's what ?" said Margaret, who had heard nothing.

"That! Don't you hear the far-off tramp of men ?"

They looked at each other fearfully. Margaret knew well enough of what Rose thought—the Bailiff and his searching party. They stopped their undressing. Nearer and nearer came that measured tread of a body of men. It paused, went on, came close under the window, and paused again. Then a thundering rattle came at the door.

"Open, in the Queen's name !"

Then they knew it had come—not the worst, but that which led to it—the beginning of the end.

Rose quietly, but quickly, put her gown on again. Before she was ready, she heard her step-father's heavy tread as he went down the stairs; heard him draw the bolt, and say, as he opened the door, in calm tones—

"Good morrow, Master Bailiff. Pray you enter with all honour, an' you come in the Queen's name."

Just then the church clock struck two. Two o'clock on the Sabbath morning!

CHAPTER XXIV

ROSE'S FIERY ORDEAL.

ART thou come, dear heart?" said Alice Mount, as her daughter ran hurriedly into her bedchamber. "That is well. Rose, the Master is come, and calleth for us, and He must find us ready."

There was no time to say more, for steps were ascending the stairs, and in another minute Master Simnel entered—the Bailiff of Colchester Hundred, whose office it was to arrest criminals within his boundaries. He was a rough, rude sort of man, from whom women were wont to shrink.

"Come, mistress, turn out!" said he. "We'll find you other lodgings for a bit."

"Master, I will do mine utmost," said Alice Mount, lifting her aching head from the pillow; "but I am now ill at ease, and I pray you, give leave for my daughter to fetch me drink ere I go hence, or I fear I may scarce walk."

We must remember that they had then no tea, coffee, or cocoa; and they had a funny idea that cold water was excessively unwholesome. The rich drank wine, and the poor thin, weak ale, most of which they brewed themselves from simple malt and hops—not at all like the strong, intoxicating stuff which people drink in public-houses now.

Mr. Simnel rather growlingly assented to the request. Rose ran down, making her way to the dresser through the rough men of whom the kitchen was full, to get a jug and a candlestick. As she came out of the kitchen, with the jug in her right hand and the candle in her left, she met a man—I believe he called himself a gentleman—named Edmund Tyrrel, a relation of that Tyrrel who had been one of the murderers of poor Edward V. and his brother. Rose dropped a courtesy, as she had been taught to do to her betters in social position.

Mr. Tyrrel stopped her. "Look thou, maid! wilt thou advise thy father and mother to be good Catholic people?"

Catholic means *general;* and for any one Church to call itself the Catholic Church, is as much as to say that it is the only Christian Church, and that other people who do not belong to it are not Christians. It is, therefore, not only untrue, but most insulting to all the Christians who belong to other Churches. St. Paul particularly warned the Church of Rome not to think herself better than other Churches, as you will see in the eleventh chapter of the Epistle to the Romans, verses 17 to 22. But she took no heed, and keeps calling herself *the* Catholic Church, as if nobody could be a Christian who did not belong to her. No Protestant Church has ever committed this sin, though some few persons in several denominations may have done so.

However, Rose was accustomed to the word, and she knew what Mr. Tyrrel meant. So she answered, gently—

"Master, they have a better instructor than I, for the Holy Ghost doth teach them, I hope, which I trust shall not suffer them to err."[1]

---

[1] This part of the story is all quite true, and I am not putting into Rose's lips, in her conversation with Mr. Tyrrel, one word which she did not really utter.

Mr. Tyrrel grew very angry. He remembered that Rose had been before the magistrates before on account of Protestant opinions.

"Why art thou still in that mind, thou naughty hussy?" cried he. "Marry, it is time to look upon such heretics indeed."

Naughty was a much stronger word then than it is now. It meant, utterly worthless and most wicked.

Brave Rose Allen! she lifted her eyes to the face of her insulter, and replied,—"Sir, with that which you call heresy, do I worship my Lord God, I tell you truth."

"Then I perceive you will burn, gossip, with the rest for company's sake," said Mr. Tyrrel, making a horrible joke.

"No, sir, not for company's sake," said Rose, "but for my Christ's sake, if so be I be compelled; and I hope in His mercies, if He call me to it, He will enable me to bear it."

Never did apostle or martyr answer better, nor bear himself more bravely, than this girl! Mr. Tyrrel was in the habit of looking with the greatest reverence on certain other young girls, whom he called Saint Agnes, Saint Margaret, and Saint Katherine—girls who had made such answers to Pagan persecutors, twelve hundred years or so before that time: but he could not see that the same scene was being enacted again, and that he was persecuting the Lord Jesus in the person of young Rose Allen. He took the candle from her hand, and she did not resist him. The next minute he was holding her firmly by the wrist, with her hand in the burning flame, watching her face to see what she would do.

She did nothing. Not a scream, not a word, not even a moan, came from the lips of Rose Allen. All that could be seen was that the empty jug which she held in the other hand trembled a little as she stood there.

" Wilt thou not cry ? " sneered Tyrrel as he held her, —and he called her some ugly names which I shall not write.

The answer was as calm as it could be. " I have no cause, thank God," said Rose tranquilly ; " but rather to rejoice. You have more cause to weep than I, if you consider the matter well."

When people set to work to vex you, nothing makes them more angry than to take it quietly, and show no vexation. That is, if they are people with mean minds. If there be any generosity in them, then it is the way to make them see that they are wrong. There was no generosity, nor love of justice, in Edmund Tyrrel. When Rose Allen stood so calmly before him, with her hand on fire, he was neither softened nor ashamed. He burned her till " the sinews began to crack," and then he let go her hand and pushed her roughly away, calling her all the bad names he could think of while he did so.

" Sir," was the meek and Christlike response, " have you done what you will do ? "

Surely few, even among martyrs, have behaved with more exquisite gentleness than this! The maiden's hand was cruelly burnt, and her tormentor was adding insult to injury by heaping false and abominable names upon her: and the worst thing she had to say to him was simply to ask whether he wished to torture her any more !

" Yes," sneered Tyrrel. " And if thou think it not well, then mend it ! "

" ' Mend it ' ! " repeated Rose. " Nay ! the Lord mend you, and give you repentance, if it be His will. And now, if you think it good, begin at the feet, and burn to the head also. For he that set you a-work shall pay you your wages one day, I warrant you."

And with this touch of sarcasm—only just enough to show how well she could have handled that weapon if she had chosen to fight with it—Rose calmly went her way, wetted a rag, and bound up her injured hand, and then drew the ale and carried it to her mother.

"How long hast thou been, child!" said her mother, who of course had no notion what had been going on downstairs.

"Ay, Mother; I am sorry for it," was the quiet reply. "Master Tyrrel stayed me in talk for divers minutes."

"What said he to thee?" anxiously demanded Alice.

"He asked me if I did mean to entreat you and my father to be good Catholics; and when I denied the same, gave me some ill words."

Rose said nothing about the burning, and as she dexterously kept her injured hand out of her mother's sight, all that Alice realized was that the girl was a trifle less quick and handy than usual.

"She's a good, quick maid in the main," said she to herself: "I'll not fault her if she's upset a bit."

While Rose was helping her mother to dress, the Bailiff was questioning her step-father whether any one else was in the house.

"I'm here," said John Thurston, rising from the pallet-bed where he lay in a corner of the little scullery. "You'd best take me, if you want me."

"Take them all!" cried Tyrrel. "They be all in one tale, be sure."

"Were you at mass this last Sunday?" said the Bailiff to Thurston. He was not quite so bad as Tyrrel

"No, that was I not," answered Thurston firmly.

"Wherefore?"

"Because I will not worship any save God Almighty."

" Why, who else would we have you to worship ? "

"Nay, it's not who else, it's what else. You would have me to worship stocks and stones, that cannot hear nor see ; and cakes of bread that the baker made overnight in his oven. I've as big a throat as other men, yet can I not swallow so great a notion as that the baker made Him that made the baker."

"Of a truth, thou art a naughty heretic !" said the Bailiff ; "and I must needs carry thee hence with the rest. But where is thy wife ?"

"Aye, where was Margaret ? Nobody had seen her since the Bailiff knocked at the door. He ordered his men to search for her ; but she had hidden herself so well that some time passed before she could be found. At length, with much laughter, one of the Bailiff's men dragged her out of a wall-closet, where she crouched hidden behind an old box. Then the Bailiff shouted for Alice Mount and Rose to be brought down, and proceeded to tie his prisoners together, two and two,— Rose contriving to slip back, so that she should be marched behind her parents.

CHAPTER XXV.

IN COLCHESTER CASTLE.

HE whole population of Much Bentley seemed to have turned out to witness the arrest at the Blue Bell. Some were kindly and sympathising, some bitter and full of taunts; but the greater number were simply inquisitive, neither friendly nor hostile, but gossipping. It was now four o'clock, a time at which half the people were up in the village, and many a woman rose an hour earlier than her wont, in order to see the strange sight. There were the carpenters with baskets of tools slung over their shoulders; the gardeners with rake or hoe; the labourers with their spades; the fishermen with their nets.

The Colne oyster-fishery is the oldest of all known fisheries in England, and its fame had reached imperial Rome itself, nearly two thousand years ago, when the Emperor Caligula came over to England partly for the purpose of tasting the Colchester oyster. The oysters are taken in the Colne and placed in pits, where they are fattened till they reach the size of a silver oyster preserved among the town treasures. In April or May, when the baby oyster first appears in the river, it looks like a drop from a tallow candle; but in twenty-four hours the shell begins to form. The value of the oyster spawn (as the baby oysters are called) in the river, is reckoned at twenty thousand pounds; and from five to ten thousand pounds' worth of oysters is sold every year.

"Well, Master Mount, how like you your new pair o' bracelets?" said one of the fishermen, as William Mount was led out, and his hands tied with a rough cord.

"Friend, I count it honour to bear for my Lord that which He first bare for me," was the meek answer.

"Father Tye 'll never preach a better word than that," said a voice in the crowd.

Mr. Simnel looked up as if to see who spoke.

"Go on with thy work, old cage-maker!" cried another voice. "We'll not find thee more gaol-birds to-day than what thou hast."

"You'd best hold your saucy tongues," said the nettled Bailiff.

"Nay, be not so tetchy, Master Simnel!" said another. The same person never seemed to speak twice; a wise precaution, since the speaker was less likely to be arrested if he did not repeat the offence. "Five slices of meat be enough for one man's supper.".

This allusion to the number of the prisoners, and the rapacity of the Bailiff, was received with laughter by the crowd. The Bailiff's temper, never of the best, was quite beyond control by this time. He relieved it by giving Mount a heavy blow, as he pushed him into line after tying his wife to him.

"Hit him back, Father Mount!" cried one of the voices.

William Mount shook his head with a smile.

"I'll hit some of you—see if I don't!" responded the incensed Bailiff, who well knew his own unpopularity.

"Hush, fellows!" said an authoritative voice. "Will ye resist the Queen's servants?"

John Thurston and his wife were next tied together, and placed behind the Mounts, the crowd remaining quiet while this was being done. Then they brought Rose Allen, and fastened her, by a cord round her wrists, to the same rope.

"Eh, Lord have mercy on the young maid!" said a woman's voice in a compassionate tone.

"Young witch, rather!" responded a man, roughly.

"Hold thy graceless tongue, Jack Milman!" replied a woman's shrill tones. "Didn't Rose Allen make broth for thee when we were both sick, and go out of a cold winter night a-gathering herbs to ease thy pain? Be shamed to thee, if thou knows what shame is, casting ill words at her in her trouble!"

Just as the prisoners were marched off, another voice hitherto silent seemed to come from the very midst of the crowd. It said,—

"Be ye faithful unto death, and Christ shall give you a crown of life."

"Take that man!" said the Bailiff, stopping.

But the man was not to be found. Nobody knew—at least nobody would own—who had uttered those fearless words.

So the prisoners were marched away on the road to Colchester. They went in at Bothal's Gate, up Bothal Street, and past the Black Friars' monastery to the Castle.

Colchester Castle is one of the oldest castles in England, for it was built by King Edward the Elder, the son of Alfred the Great. It is a low square mass, with the largest Norman keep, or centre tower, in the country. The walls are twelve feet thick, and the whole ground floor, and two of the four towers, are built up perfectly solid from the bottom, that it might be made as strong as possible. It was built with Roman bricks, and the Roman mortar still sticks to some of them. Builders always know Roman mortar, for it is so much harder than any mortar people know how to make now —quite as hard as stone itself. The chimneys run up through the walls.

The prisoners were marched up to the great entrance gate, on the south side of the Castle. The Bailiff blew his horn, and the porter opened a little wicket and looked out.

"Give you good morrow, Master Bailiff. Another batch, I reckon?"

"Ay, another batch, belike. You'll have your dungeons full ere long."

"Oh, we've room enough and to spare!" said the porter with a grin. "None so many, yet. Two men fetched in yestereven for breaking folks' heads in a drunken brawl; and two or three debtors; and a lad for thieving, and such; then Master Maynard brought an handful in this morrow—Moot Hall was getting too full, he said."

"Aye so? who brought he?"

"Oh, Alegar o' Thorpe, and them bits o' children o' his, that should be learning their hornbooks i' school sooner than be here, trow."

"You'd best teach 'em, Tom," suggested Mr. Simnel with a grim smile. "Now then, in with you!"

And the prisoners were marched into the Castle dungeon.

In the corner of the dungeon sat John Johnson, his Bible on his knee, and beside him, snuggled close to him, Cissy. Little Will was seated on the floor at his father's feet, playing with some bits of wood. Johnson looked up as his friends entered.

"Why, good friends! Shall I say I am glad or sorry to behold you here?"

"Glad," answered William Mount, firmly, "if so we may glorify God."

"I'm glad, I know," said Cissy, jumping from the form, and giving a warm hug to Rose. "I thought God would send somebody. You see, Father was down a bit when we came here this morning, and left everybody behind us; but you've come now, and he'll be ever so pleased. It isn't bad, you know—not bad at all—and then there's Father. But, Rose, what have you done to your hand? It's tied up."

"Hush, dear! Only hurt it a bit, Cissy. Don't speak of it," said Rose in an undertone; "I don't want mother to see it, or she'll trouble about it, maybe. It doesn't hurt much now."

Cissy nodded, with a face which said that she thoroughly entered into Rose's wish for silence.

"Eh dear, dear! that we should have lived to see this day!" cried Margaret Thurston, melting into tears as she sat down in the corner.

"Rose!" said her father suddenly, "thy left hand is bound up. Hast hurt it, maid?"

Rose's eyes, behind her mother's back, said, "Please don't ask me anything about it!" But Alice turned round to look, and she had to own the truth.

"Why, maid! That must have been by the closet where I was hid, and I never heard thee scream," said Margaret.

"Nay, Meg, I screamed not."

"Lack-a-day! how could'st help the same?"

"Didn't it hurt sore, Rose?" asked John Thurston.

"Not nigh so much as you might think," answered Rose, brightly. "At the first it caused me some grief; but truly, the more it burned the less it hurt, till at last it was scarce any hurt at all."

"But thou had'st the pot in thine other hand, maid;

wherefore not have hit him a good swing there-with?"

"Truly, Meg, I thank God that He held mine hand from any such deed. 'The servant of the Lord must not strive.' I should thus have dishonoured my Master."

"Marry, but that may be well enough for angels and such like. *We* dwell in this nether world."

"Rose hath the right," said William Mount. "We may render unto no man railing for railing. 'If we suffer as Christians, happy are we; for the Spirit of glory and of God resteth upon us.' Let us not suffer as malefactors."

"You say well, neighbour," added John Thurston. "We be called to the defence of God's truth, but in no wise to defend ourselves."

"Nay, the Lord is the avenger of all that have none other," said Alice. "But let me see thine hand, child, maybe I can do thee some ease."

"Under your good leave, Mother, I would rather not unlap it," replied Rose. "Truly, it scarce doth me any hurt now; and I bound it well with a wet rag, that I trow it were better to let it be. It shall do well enough, I cast no doubt."

She did not want her mother to see how terribly it was burned. And in her heart was a further thought which she would not put into words—If they shortly burn my whole body, what need is there to trouble about this little hurt to my hand?

CHAPTER XXVI.

SHUTTING THE DOOR.

NCE more the days wore on, and no fresh arrests were made; but no help came to the prisoners in the Castle and the Moot Hall, nor to Elizabeth Foulkes in the keeping of Mr. Ashby. Two priests had talked to Elizabeth, and the authorities were beginning to change their opinion about her. They had fancied from her quiet, meek appearance, that she would be easily prevailed upon to say what they wanted. Now they found that under that external softness there was a will of iron, and a power of endurance beyond anything they had imagined.

The day of examination for all the prisoners—the last day, when they would be sentenced or acquitted—was appointed to be the 23rd of June. On the previous day the Commissioners called Elizabeth Foulkes before them. She came, accompanied by Mr. Ashby and her uncle; and they asked her only one question.

"Dost thou believe in a Catholic Church of Christ, or no?"

Of course Elizabeth replied "Yes," for the Bible has plenty to say of the Church of Christ, though it never identifies it with the Church of Rome. They asked her no more, for Boswell, the scribe, interposed, and begged that she might be consigned to the keeping of her uncle. The Commissioners assented, and Holt took her away,

It looks very much as if Boswell had wanted her to escape. She was much more carelessly guarded in her uncle's house than in Mr. Ashby's, and could have got away easily enough if she had chosen. She was more than once sent to open the front door, whence she might have slipped out after dark with almost a certainty of escape. It was quite dark when she answered the last rap.

"Pray you," asked an old man's voice, "is here a certain young maid, by name Elizabeth Foulkes?"

"I am she, master. What would you with me?"

"A word apart," he answered in a whisper. "Be any ears about that should not be?"

Elizabeth glanced back into the kitchen where her aunt was sewing, and her two cousins gauffering the large ruffs which both men and women then wore.

"None that can harm. Say on, my master."

"Bessy, dost know my voice?"

"I do somewhat, yet I can scarce put a name thereto."

"I am Walter Purcas, of Bocking."

"Robin's father! Ay, I know you well now, and I cry you mercy that I did no sooner."

"Come away with me, Bessy!" he said, in a loud whisper. "I have walked all the way from Bocking to see if I might save thee, for Robin's sake, for he loves thee as he loveth nought else save me. Mistress Wade shall lend me an horse, and we can be safe ere night be o'er, in the house of a good man that I know in a place unsuspect. O Bessy, my dear lass, save thyself and come with me!"

"Save thyself!" The words had been addressed once before, fifteen hundred years back, to One who did not save Himself, because He came to save the world. Before the eyes of Elizabeth rose two visions —one fair and sweet enough, a vision of safety and comfort, of life and happiness, which might be yet in state for her. But it was blotted out by the other—a vision of three crosses reared on a bare rock, when the One who hung in the midst could have saved Himself at the cost of the glory of the Father and the everlasting bliss of His Church. And from that cross a voice seemed to whisper to her—"If any man serve Me, let him follow Me."

"Verily, I am loth you should have your pain for nought," said she, "but indeed I cannot come with you, though I do thank you with all my heart. I am set here in ward of mine uncle, and for me to 'scape away would cause penalty to fall on him. I cannot save myself at his cost. And should not the Papists take it to mean that I had not the courage to stand to that which they demanded of me? Nay, Father Purcas, this will I not do, for so should I lose my crown, and dim the glory of my Christ."

"Bessy!" cried her aunt from the kitchen, "do come within and shut the door, maid! Here's the wind a-blowing in till I'm nigh feared o' losing my ears, and all the lace like to go up the chimney, while thou tarriest chatting yonder. What gossip hast thou there? Canst thou not bring her in?"

"Bessy, *come!*" whispered Purcas earnestly.

But Elizabeth shook her head. "The Lord bless you! I dare not." And she shut the door, knowing that by so doing, she virtually shut it upon life and happiness—that is, happiness in this life. Elizabeth went quietly back to the kitchen, and took up an iron. She scarcely knew what she was ironing, nor how she answered her cousin Dorothy's rather sarcastic observations upon the interesting conversation which she seemed to have had. A few minutes later her eldest cousin, a married woman, who lived in a neighbouring street, lifted the latch and came in.

"Good even, Mother!" said she. "Well, Doll, and
Jenny! So thou gave in at last, Bess? I'm fain for
thee. It's no good fighting against a stone wall."

"What dost thou mean, Chrissy?"

"What mean I? Why, didn't thou give in? Lots
o' folks is saying so. Set thy name, they say, to a
paper that thou'd yield to the Pope, and be obedient in
all things. I hope it were true."

"True! that I yielded to the Pope, and promised
to obey him!" cried Elizabeth in fiery indignation.
"It's not true, Christian Meynell! Tell every soul so
that asks thee! I'll die before I do it. Where be the
Commissioners?"

"Thank the saints, they've done their sitting," said
Mrs. Meynell, laughing: "or I do believe this foolish
maid should run right into the lion's den. Mother,
lock her up to-morrow, won't you, without she's summoned?"

"Where are they?" peremptorily demanded Elizabeth.

"Sitting down to their supper at Mistress Cosin's,"
was the laughing answer. "Don't thou spoil it by
rushing in all of a——"

"I shall go to them this minute," said Elizabeth
tying on her hood, which she had taken down from its
nail. "No man nor woman shall say such words of me.
Good-night, Aunt; I thank you for all your goodness,
and may the good Lord bless you and yours for ever
Farewell!" And amid a shower of exclamations and en-
treaties from her startled relatives, who never expected
conduct approaching to this, Elizabeth left the house.

She had not far to go on that last walk in this world.
The White Hart, where the Commissioners were staying,
was full of light and animation that night when she
stepped into it from the dark street, and asked leave
to speak a few words to the Queen's Commissioners,

"What would you with them?" asked a red-cheeked maid who came to her.

"That shall they know speedily," was the answer.

The Commissioners were rather amused to be told that a girl wanted to see them: but when they heard who it was, they looked at each other with raised eyebrows, and ordered her to be called in. They had finished supper, and were sitting over their wine, as gentlemen were then wont to do rather longer than was good for them.

Elizabeth came forward to the table and confronted them. The Commissioners themselves were two in number, Sir John Kingston and Dr. Chedsey; but the scribe, sheriff, and bailiffs were also present.

"Worshipful Sirs," she said in a clear voice, "I have been told it is reported in this town that I have made this day by you submission and obedience to the Pope. And since this is not true, nor by God's grace shall never be, I call on you to do your duty, and commit me to the Queen's Highness' prison, that I may yet again bear my testimony for my Lord Christ."

There was dead silence for a moment. Dr. Chedsey looked at the girl with admiration which seemed almost reverence. Sir John Kingston knit his brows, and appeared inclined to examine her there and then. Boswell half rose as if he would once more have pleaded with or for her. But Maynard, the Sheriff, whom nothing touched, and who was scarcely sober, sprang to his feet and dashed his hand upon the table, with a cry that "the jibbing jade should repent kicking over the traces this time!" He seized Elizabeth, marched her to the Moot Hall, and thrust her into the dungeon: and with a bass clang as if it had been the very gate of doom, the great door closed behind her.

CHAPTER XXVII.

AT THE BAR.

HE great hall of the Moot Hall in Colchester was filling rapidly. Every townsman, and every townswoman, wanted to hear the examination, and to know the fate of the prisoners—of whom there were so many that not many houses were left in Colchester where the owners had not some family connection or friend among them. Into the hall, robed in judicial ermine, filed the Royal Commissioners, Sir John Kingston, and Dr. Chedsey, followed by Boswell, the scribe, Robert Maynard and Robert Brown the Sheriffs, several priests, and many magistrates and gentlemen of the surrounding country. Having opened the Court, they first summoned before them William Bongeor, the glazier, of St. Michael's parish, aged sixty, then Thomas Benold, the tallow-chandler, and thirdly, Robert Purcas.

They asked Purcas "what he had to say touching the Sacrament."

"When we receive the Sacrament," he answered, "we receive bread in an holy use, that preacheth remembrance that Christ died for us."

The three men were condemned to death: and then Agnes Silverside was brought to the bar. She was some time under examination, for she answered all the questions asked her so wisely and so firmly, that the

Commissioners themselves were disconcerted. They took refuge, as such men usually did, in abuse, calling her ugly names, and asking "if she wished to burn her rotten old bones ?"

Helen Ewring, the miller's wife, followed : and both were condemned.

Then the last of the Moot Hall prisoners, Elizabeth Foulkes, was placed at the bar.

"Dost thou believe," inquired Dr. Chedsey, "that in the most holy Sacrament of the altar, the body and blood of Christ is really and substantially present?"

Elizabeth's reply, in her quiet, clear voice, was audible in every part of the hall.

"I believe it to be a substantial lie, and a real lie."

"Shame ! shame !" cried one of the priests on the bench.

"Horrible blasphemy !" cried another.

"What is it, then, that there is before consecration ?" asked Dr. Chedsey.

"Bread."

"Well said. And what is there after consecration?"

"Bread, still."

"Nothing more ?"

"Nothing more," said Elizabeth firmly. "The receiving of Christ lies not in the bread, but is heavenly and spiritual only."

"What say you to confession ? "

'I will use none, seeing no priest hath power to remit sin."

"Will you go to mass ? "

"I will not, for it is idolatry."

"Will you submit to the authority of the Pope ? "

Elizabeth's answer was even stronger than before.

"I do utterly detest all such trumpery from the bottom of my heart ! "

They asked her no more. Dr. Chedsey, for the sixth and last time, assumed the black cap, and read the sentence of death.

"Thou shalt be taken from here to the place whence thou camest, and thence to the place of execution, there to be burned in the fire till thou art dead."

Never before had Chedsey's voice been known to falter in pronouncing that sentence. He had spoken it to white-haired men, and delicate women, ay, even to little children; but this once, every spectator looked up in amazement at his tone, and saw the judge in tears. And then, turning to the prisoner, they saw her face "as it were the face of an angel."

Before any one could recover from the sudden hush of awe which had fallen upon the Court, Elizabeth Foulkes knelt down, and carried her appeal from that unjust sentence to the higher bar of God Almighty.

"O Lord our Father!" she said, "I thank and praise and glorify Thee that I was ever born to see this day— this most blessed and happy day, when Thou hast accounted me worthy to suffer for the testimony of Christ. And, Lord, if it be Thy will, forgive them that thus have done against me, for they know not what they do."

How many of us would be likely to thank God for allowing us to be martyrs? These were true martyrs who did so, men and women so full of the Holy Ghost that they counted not their lives dear unto them,—so upheld by God's power that the shrinking of the flesh from that dreadful pain and horror was almost forgotten. We must always remember that it was not by their own strength, or their own goodness, but by the blood of the Lamb, that Christ's martyrs have triumphed over death and Satan.

Then Elizabeth rose from her knees, and turned towards the Bench. Like an inspired prophetess she spoke—this poor, simple, humble servant-girl of twenty years—astonishing all who heard her.

"Repent, all ye that sit there!" she cried earnestly, "and especially ye that brought me to this prison: above all thou, Robert Maynard, that art so careless of human life that thou wilt oft sit sleeping on the bench when a man is tried for his life. Repent, O ye halting Gospellers! and beware of blood-guiltiness, for that shall call for vengeance. Yea, if ye will not herein repent your wicked doings."—and as Elizabeth spoke, she laid her hand upon the bar—"this very bar shall be witness against you in the Day of Judgment, that ye have this day shed innocent blood!"

Oh, how England needs such a prophetess now! and above all, those "halting Gospellers," the men who talk sweetly about charity and toleration, and sit still, and will not come to the help of the Lord against the mighty! They sorely want reminding that Christ has said, "He that is not with us is against us." It is a very poor excuse to say, "Oh, I am not doing any harm." Are you doing any good? That is the question. If not, a wooden post is as good as you are. And are you satisfied to be no better than a wooden post?

What grand opportunities there are before boys and girls on the threshold of life! What are you going to do with your life? Remember, you have only one. And there are only two things you can do with it. You must give it to somebody—and it must be either God or Satan. All the lives that are not given to God fall into the hands of Satan. There are very few people who say to themselves deliberately, Now, I will not give my life to God. They only say, Oh, there's plenty of time; I won't do it just now; I want to enjoy myself. They don't know that there is no happiness on earth like that of deciding for God. And so they go on day after day, not deciding either way, but just frittering their lives away bit by bit, until the last day comes, and the last bit of life, and then it is too late to decide. Would you like such a poor, mean, valueless thing as this to be the one life which is all you have? Would you not rather have a bright, rich, full life, with God Himself for your best friend on earth, and then a triumphal entry into the Golden City, and the singer's harp, and the victor's palm, and the prince's crown, and the King's "Well done, good and faithful servant"?

Do you say, Yes. I would choose that, but I do not know how? Well, then, tell the Lord that. Say to Him, "Lord, I want to be Thy friend and servant, and I do not know how." Keep on saying it till He shows you how. He is sure to do it, for He cares about it much more than you do. Never fancy for one minute that God does not want you to go to Heaven, and that it will be hard work to persuade Him to let you in. He wants you to come more than you want it. He gave His own Son that you might come. "Greater love hath no man than this."

Now, will you not come to Him—will you not say to Him, "Lord, here am I; take me"? Are you going to let the Lord Jesus feel that all the cruel suffering which He bore for you was in vain? He is ready to save you, if you will let Him; but He will not do it against your will. How shall it be?

CHAPTER XXVIII.

THE SONG OF TRIUMPH.

LIZABETH FOULKES was the last prisoner tried in the Moot Hall. The Commissioners then adjourned to the Castle. Here there were six prisoners, as before. The first arraigned was William Mount. He was asked, as they all were—it was the great test question for the Marian martyrs—what he had to say of the Sacrament of the altar, which was another name for the mass.

"I say that it is an abominable idol," was his answer.

"Wherefore comest thou not to confession?"

"Sirs, I dare not take part in any Popish doings, for fear of God's vengeance," said the brave old man.

Brave! ay, for the penalty was death. But what are they, of whom there are so many, whose actions if not words say that they dare not refuse to take part in Popish doings, for fear of man's scorn and ridicule? Poor, mean cowards!

It was not worth while to go further. William Mount was sentenced to death, and John Johnson was brought to the bar. Neither were they long with him, for he had nothing to say but what he had said before. He too was sentenced to die.

Then Alice Mount was brought up. She replied to

their questions exactly as her husband had done. She was satisfied with his answers: they should be hers. Once more the sentence was read, and she was led away.

Then Rose Allen was placed at the bar. So little had the past daunted her, that she did more than defy the Commissioners: she made fun of them. Standing there with her burnt hand still in its wrappings, she positively laughed Satan and all his servants to scorn.

They asked her what she had to say touching the mass.

"I say that it stinketh in the face of God![1] and I dare not have to do therewith for my life.'

"Are you not a member of the Catholic Church?"

"I am no member of yours, for ye be members of Antichrist, and shall have the reward of Antichrist."

"What say you of the see of the Bishop of Rome?"

"I am none of his. As for his see, it is for crows, kites, owls, and ravens to swim in, such as you be; for by the grace of God I will not swim in that sea while I live, neither will I have any thing to do therewith."

Nothing could overcome the playful wit of this indomitable girl. She punned on their words, she laughed at their threats, she held them up to ridicule. This must be ended.

For the fourth time Dr. Chedsey assumed the black cap. Rose kept silence while she was condemned to death. But no sooner had his voice ceased than, to

---

[1] Rose's words are given as she spoke them: but it must be remembered that they would not sound nearly so strong to those who heard them as they do to us.

the amazement of all who heard her, she broke forth
into song. It was verily

> "The shout of them that triumph,
> The song of them that feast."

She was led out of the court and down the dungeon steps, singing, till her voice filled the whole
court.

> "Yea, though I walk through death's dark vale,
> Yet will I fear none ill;
> Thy rod, Thy staff doth comfort me,
> And Thou art with me still."

Which was the happier, do you think, that night?
Dr. Chedsey, who had read the sentence of death upon
ten martyrs? or young Rose Allen, who was to be
burned to death in five weeks?

When Rose's triumphant voice had died away, the
gaoler was hastily bidden to bring the other two
prisoners. The Commissioners were very much an-
noyed. It was a bad thing for the people who stood
by, they thought, when martyrs insisted on singing
in response to a sentence of execution. They wanted
to make the spectators forget such scenes.

"Well, where be the prisoners?" said Sir John
Kingston.

"Please, your Worships, they be at the bar!"
answered the gaolor, with a grin.

"At the bar, man?   But I see nought. Be they
dwarfs?"

"Something like," said the gaoler.

He dragged up a form to the bar, and lifted on it,
first, Will Johnson, and then Cissy.

"Good lack! such babes as these!" said Sir John,
in great perplexity.

He felt it really very provoking. Here was a girl

of twenty who had made fun of him in the most merciless manner, and had the audacity to sing when condemned to die, thus setting a shocking example, and awakening the sympathy of the public : and here, to make matters worse, were two little children brought up as heretics ! This would never do. It was the more awkward from his point of view, that Cissy was so small that he took her to be much younger than she was.

"I cannot examine these babes !" said he to Chedsey.

Dr. Chedsey, in answer, took the examination on himself.

" How old art thou, my lad ? " said he to Will.

Will made no answer, and his sister spoke up for him.

" Please, sir, he's six."

" And what dost thou believe ? " asked the Commissioner, half scornfully, half amused.

"Please, we believe what Father told us."

"Who is their father ? " was asked of the gaoler.

" Johnson, worshipful Sirs : Alegar, of Thorpe, that you have sentenced this morrow."

" Gramercy ! " said Sir John. " Take them down, Wastborowe,—take them down, and carry them away. Have them up another day. Such babes ! "

Cissy heard him, and felt insulted, as a young woman of her age naturally would.

" Please, Sir, I'm not a baby ! Baby's a baby, but Will's six, and I'm going in ten. And we are going to be as good as we can, and mind all Father said to us."

" Take them away—take them away ! " cried Sir John.

Wastborowe lifted Will down.

"But please——" said Cissy piteously—"isn't nothing to be done to us? Mayn't we go 'long of Father?"

"Ay, for the present," answered Wastborowe, as he took a hand of each to lead them back.

"But isn't Father to be burned?"

"Come along! I can't stay," said the gaoler hastily. Even his hard heart shrank from answering yes to that little pleading face.

"But please, oh please, they mustn't burn Father and not us! We *must* go with Father."

"Wastborowe!" Sir John's voice called back.

'Take 'em down, Tom," said Wastborowe to his man,—not at all sorry to go away from Cissy. He ran back to court.

"We are of opinion, Wastborowe," said Dr. Chedsey rather pompously, "that these children are too young and ignorant to be put to the bar. We make order, therefore, that they be discharged, and set in care of some good Catholic woman, if any be among their kindred; and if not, let them be committed to the care of some such not akin to them."

"Please, your Worships, I know nought of their kindred," said the gaoler scratching his head. "Jane Hiltoft hath the babe at this present."

"What, is there a lesser babe yet?" asked Dr. Chedsey, laughing.

"Ay, there is so: a babe in arms."

"Worshipful Sirs, might it please you to hear a poor woman?"

"Speak on, good wife."

"Sirs," said the woman who had spoken, coming forward out of the crowd, "my name is Ursula Felstede, and I dwell at Thorpe- the next door to Johnson. The babes know me, and have been in my charge aforetime.

May I pray your good Worships to set them in my care? I have none of mine own, and would bring them up to mine utmost as good subjects and honest folks."

"Ay so? and how about good Catholics?"

"Sirs, Father Tye will tell you I go to mass and confession both."

"So she doth," said the priest: "but I misdoubt somewhat if she be not of the 'halting Gospellers' whereof we heard this morrow in the Moot Hall."

"Better put them in charge of the Black Sisters of Hedingham," suggested Dr. Chedsey. "Come you this even, good woman, to the White Hart, and you shall then hear our pleasure. Father Tye, I pray you come with us to supper."

Dr. Chedsey had quite recovered from his emotions of the morning.

"Meanwhile," said Sir John, rising, "let the morrow of Lammas[1] be appointed for the execution of those sentenced."

---

[1] The second of August.

CHAPTER XXIX.

MAN PROPOSES.

RS. COSIN, the landlady of the White Hart, prepared a very good supper for the Commissioners. These gentlemen did not fare badly. First, they had a dish of the oysters for which the town was famous, then some roast beef and a big venison pasty, then some boiled pigeons, then two or three puddings, a raspberry pie, curds and whey, cheese, with a good deal of Malmsey wine and old sack, finishing up with cherries and sweet biscuits.

They had reached the cherry stage before they began to talk beyond mere passing remarks. Then the priest said :—

"I am somewhat feared, Master Commissioners, you shall reckon Colchester an infected place, seeing there be here so many touched with the poison of heresy."

"It all comes of self-conceit," said Sir John.

"Nay," answered Dr. Chedsey. "Self-conceit is scarce wont to bring a man to the stake. It were more like to save him from it."

"Well, but why can't they let things alone?" inquired Sir John, helping himself to a biscuit. "They know well enough what they shall come to if they meddle with matters of religion. Why don't they leave the priest to think for them?"

Dr. Chedsey was silent: not because he did not know the answer. The time was when he, too, had been one of those now despised and condemned Gospellers. In Edward the Sixth's day, he had preached the full, rich Gospel of the grace of God : and now he was a deserter to the enemy. Some of such men—perhaps most—grew very hard and stony, and seemed to take positive pleasure in persecuting those who were more faithful than themselves: but there were a few with whom the Spirit of God continued to strive, who now and then remembered from whence they had fallen, and to whom that remembrance brought poignant anguish when it came upon them. Dr. Chedsey appears to have been one of this type. Let us hope that these wandering sheep came home at last in the arms of the Good Shepherd who sought them with such preserving tenderness. But the sad truth is that we scarcely know with certainty of one who did so. On the accession of Elizabeth, when we might have expected them to come forward and declare their repentance if it were sincere, they did no such thing : they simply dropped into oblivion, and we lose them there.

It is a hard and bitter thing to depart from God : how hard, and how bitter, only those know in this world who try to turn round and come back. It will be known fully in that other world whence there is no coming back.

Dr. Chedsey, then, was silent : not because he did not understand the matter, but because he knew it too well. Sir John had said the Protestants "knew what they would come to " : that was the stake and the fire. But those who persecuted Christ in the person of His elect—what were they going to come to ? It was not pleasant to think about that. Dr. Chedsey was very glad that it was just then announced that a woman begged leave to speak with their Worships.

"It shall be yon woman that would fain take the children, I cast no doubt," said Sir John: "and we have had no talk thereupon. Shall she have them or no?"

"What say you, Father Tye?"

"Truly, that I have not over much trust in Felstede's wife. She was wont of old time to have Bible readings and prayer-meetings at her house; and though she feigneth now to be reconciled and Catholic, yet I doubt her repentance is but skin deep. The children were better a deal with the Black Nuns. Yet—there may be some time ere we can despatch them thither, and if you thought good, Felstede's wife might have them till then."

"Good!" said Sir John. "Call the woman in."

Ursula Felstede was called in, and stood curtesying at the door. Sir John put on his stern and pompous manner in speaking to her.

"It seemeth best to the Queen's Grace's Commission," said he, "that these children were sent in the keeping of the Sisters of Hedingham: yet as time may elapse ere the Prioress cometh to town, we leave them in thy charge until she send for them. Thou shalt keep them well, learn them to be good Catholics, and deliver them to the Black Nuns when they demand it."

Ursula courtesied again, and "hoped she should do her duty."

"So do I hope," said the priest. "But I give thee warning, Ursula Felstede, that thy duty hath not been over well done ere this: and 'tis high time thou shouldst amend if thou desire not to be brought to book."

Urusla dropped half-a-dozen courtesies in a flurried way.

"Please it, your Reverence, I am a right true Catholic, and shall learn the children so to be."

"Mind thou dost!" said Sir John.

Dr. Chedsey meanwhile had occupied himself in writ-

ing out an order for the children to be delivered to
Ursula, to which he affixed the seal of the Commission.
Armed with this paper, and having taken leave of the
Commissioners, with many protests that she would "do
her duty," Ursula made her way to the Castle gate.

" Who walks so late ? " asked the porter, looking out
of his little wicket to see who it was.

"Good den, Master Style. I am James Felstede's
wife of Thorpe, and I come with an order from their
Worships the Commissioners to take Johnson's children
to me ; they be to dwell in my charge till the Black
Sisters shall send for them."

"Want 'em to-night ? " asked the porter rather gruffly.

"Well, what say you ?—are they abed ? I'm but a
poor woman, and cannot afford another walk from
Thorpe. I'd best take 'em with me now."

"You're never going back to Thorpe to-night?"

"Well, nay. I'm going to tarry the night at my
brother's outside East Gate."

"Bless the woman ! then call for the children in the
morning, and harry not honest folk out o' their lives at
bedtime."

And Style dashed the wicket to.

"Now, then, Kate! be those loaves ready? The
rogues shall be clamouring for their suppers," cried he
to his wife.

Katherine Style, who baked the prison bread, brought
out in answer a large tray, on which three loaves of bread
were cut in thick slices, with a piece of cheese and a
bunch of radishes laid on each. These were for the supper
of the prisoners. Style shouted for the gaoler, and he
came up and carried the tray into the dungeon, followed
by the porter, who was in rather a funny mood, and—
as I am sorry to say is often the case—was not, in his
fun, careful of other people's feelings.

"Now, Johnson, hast thou done with those children?" said he. "Thou'd best make thy last dying speech and confession to 'em, for they're going away to-morrow morning."

Johnson looked up with a grave, white face. Little Cissy, who was sitting by Rose Allen, at once ran to her father, and twined her arm in his, with an uneasy idea of being parted from him, though she did not clearly understand what was to happen.

"Where?" was all Johnson seemed able to say.

"Black Nuns o' Hedingham," said the porter. He did not say anything about the temporary sojourn with Ursula Felstede.

Johnson groaned and drew Cissy closer to him.

"Don't be feared, Father," said Cissy bravely, though her lips quivered till she could hardly speak. "Don't be feared: we'll never do anything you've told us not."

"God bless thee, my darling, and God help thee!" said the poor father. "Little Cissy, He must be thy Father now." And looking upwards, he said, "Lord, take the charge that I give into Thine hands this night! Be Thou the Father to these fatherless little ones, and lead them forth by a smooth way or a rough, so it be the right way, whereby they shall come to Thy holy hill, and to Thy tabernacle. Keep them as the apple of Thine eye; hide them under the covert of Thy wings! I am no more in the world; but these are in the world: keep them through Thy Name. Give them back safe to my Helen and to me in the land that is very far off, whereinto there shall enter nothing that defileth. Lord, I trust them to no man, but only unto Thee! Here me, O Lord my God, for I rest on Thee. Let no man prevail against Thee. I have no might against this company that cometh against me, neither know I what to do: but mine eyes are upon Thee."

CHAPTER XXX.

HAT! Agnes Bongeor taken to the Moot Hall? Humph! they'll be a-coming for me next. I must get on with my work. Let's do as much as we can for the Lord, ere we're called to suffer for Him. Thou tookest my message to Master Commissary, Doll?"

Dorothy Denny murmured something which did not reach the ear of Mrs. Wade.

"Speak up, woman! I say, thou tookest my message?"

"Well, Mistress, I thought——"

"A fig for thy thought! Didst give my message touching Johnson's children?"

"N—o, Mistress, I,——"

"Beshrew thee for an unfaithful messenger. Dost know what the wise King saith thereof? He says it is like a foot out of joint. Hadst ever thy foot out o' joint? I have, and I tell thee, if thou hadst the one foot out of joint, thou wouldst not want t'other. I knew well thou wert an ass, but I did not think thee unfaithful. Why didst not give my message?"

There were tears in Dorothy's eyes.

"Mistress," said she, "forgive me, but I will not help you to run into trouble, though you're sore set to do it. It shall serve no good purpose to keep your

name for ever before the eyes of Master Commissary
and his fellows. Do, pray, let them forget you. You'll
ne'er be safe, an' you thrust yourself forward thus."

"Safe! Bless the woman! I leave the Lord to see
to my safety. I've no care but to get His work done."

"Well, then He's the more like to have a care of
you; but, Mistress, won't you let Dorothy Denny try to
see to you a bit too?"

"Thou'rt a good maid, Doll, though I'm a bit sharp
on thee at times; and thou knows thou art mortal slow.
Howbeit, tell me, what is come of those children? If
they be in good hands, I need not trouble."

"Ursula Felstede has them, Mistress, till the Black
Nuns of Hedingham shall fetch them away."

"Ursula Felstede! 'Unstable as water.' That for
Ursula Felstede. Black Nuns shall not have 'em while
Philippa Wade's above ground. I tell thee, Dorothy,
wherever those little ones go, the Lord's blessing 'll go
with them. Dost mind what David saith? 'I have
been young, and now am old; and yet saw I never the
righteous forsaken, nor his seed begging their bread.'
And I want them, maid,—part because I feel for the
little ones, and part because I want the blessing. Why,
that poor little Cicely 'll be crying her bits of eyes out
to part with 'Father.' Doll, I'll go down this even, if
I may find leisure, to Ursula Felstede, and see if I cannot win her to give me the children. I shall tell her
my mind first, as like as not: and much good may it do
her! But I'll have a try for 'em—I will."

"Folks saith, Mistress, the prisoners be in as good
case as may be: always reading and strengthening one
another, and praising God."

"I'm fain to hear it, Dorothy. Ah, they be not the
worst off in this town. If the Lord were to come to
judge the earth this even, I'd a deal liefer be one of

them in the Moot Hall than be of them that have them
in charge. I marvel He comes not. If he had been a
man and not God, He'd have been down many a time
afore now."

About six o'clock on a hot July evening, Ursula Felstede heard a tap at her door.

"Come in! O Mistress Wade, how do you do? Will
you sit? I'm sure you're very welcome," said Ursula,
in some confusion.

"I'm not quite so sure of it, Ursula Felstede: but let
be. You've Johnson's children here, haven't you?"

"Ay, I have so: and I tell you that Will's a handful!
Seems to me he's worser to rule than he used. He's
getting bigger, trow."

"And Cicely?"

"Oh, she's quiet enough, only a bit obstinate. Won't
always do as she's told. I have to look after her sharp,
or she'd be off, I do believe."

"I'd like to see her, an't please you."

"Well, to be sure! I sent 'em out to play them a
bit. I don't just know where they are."

"Call that looking sharp after 'em?"

Ursula laughed a little uneasily.

"Well, one can't be just a slave to a pack of children,
can one? I'll look out and see if they are in sight."

"Thank you, I'll do that, without troubling you.
Now, Ursula Felstede, I've one thing to say to you, so
I'll say it and get it over. Those children of Johnson's
have the Lord's wings over them: they'll be taken care
of, be sure: but if you treat them ill, or if you meddle
with what their father learned them, you'll have to
reckon with Him instead of the Queen's Commissioners.
And I'd a deal sooner have the Commissioners against
me than have the Lord. Be not afraid of them that kill
the body, and after that have no more that they can do:

but fear Him which after He hath killed, hath power to cast into Hell. Yea, I say unto thee, Fear Him!"

And Mrs. Wade walked out of the door without saying another word. She was going to look for the children. The baby she had already seen asleep on Ursula's bed. Little Will she found in the midst of a group of boys down by the brook, one of whom, a lad twice his size, was just about to fight him when Mrs. Wade came up.

"Now, Jack Tyler, if thou dost not want to be carried to thy father by the scuff of thy neck, like a cat, and well thrashed to end with, let that lad alone.—Will, where's thy sister?"

Little Will, who looked rather sheepish, said,—

"Over there."

"Where's *there?*"

"On the stile. She's always there when we're out, except she's looking after me."

"Thou lackest looking after."

"Philip Tye said he'd see to me: and then he went off with Jem Morris, bird-nesting."

"Cruel lads! well, you're a proper lot! It'd do you good, and me too, to give you a caning all round. I shall have to let be to-night, for I want to find Cicely."

"Well, you'll see her o' top o' the stile."

Little Will turned back to his absorbing amusement of bulrush-plaiting, and Mrs. Wade went up to the stile which led to the way over the fields towards Colchester. As she came near, sheltered by the hedge, she heard a little voice.

> " Yea, though I walk in vale of death,
>   Yet will I fear no ill:
> Thy rod, Thy staff, doth comfort me,
>   And Thou art with me still."

Mrs. Wade crept softly along till she could see through

the hedge. The stile was a stone one, with steps on each side, such as may still be seen in the north of England : and on the top step sat Cissy, resting her head upon her hand, and looking earnestly in the direction of Colchester.

"What dost there, my dear heart ?" Mrs. Wade asked gently.

"I'm looking at Father," said Cissy, rather languidly. She spoke as if she were not well, and could not care much about anything.

"'Looking at Father'! What dost thou mean, my child ?"

"Well, you see that belt of trees over yonder ? When the sun shines, I can see All Hallows' tower stand up against it. You can't see it to-day : it does not shine ; but it's there for all that. And Father's just behind in the Castle : so I haven't any better way to look at him. Only God looks at him, you know ; they can't bar Him out. So I come here, and look as far as I can, and talk to God about Father. I can't see Father, but he's there : and I can't see God, but He's there too : and He's got to see to Father now I can't."

The desolate tone of utter loneliness in the little voice touched Mrs. Wade to the core of her great warm heart.

"My poor little Cicely !" she said. "Doth Ursula use thee well ?"

"Yes, I suppose so," said Cissy, in a quiet matter-of-fact way ; "only when I won't pray to her big image, she slaps me. But she can't make me do it. Father said not. It would never do for God to see us doing things Father forbade us, because he's shut up and can't come to us. I'm not going to pray to that ugly thing : never ! And if it was pretty, it wouldn't make any difference, when Father said not. '

" No, dear heart, that were idolatry," said Mrs. Wade.

" Yes, I know," replied Cissy : " Father said so. But Ursula says the Black Sisters will make me, or they'll put me in the well. I do hope God will keep away the Black Sisters. I ask Him every day, when I've done talking about Father. I shouldn't like them to put me in the well !" and she shuddered. Evidently Ursula had frightened her very much with some story about this. " But God would be there, in the well, wouldn't He ? They won't make me do it when Father said not !"

CHAPTER XXXI

SUMPTUOUS APARTMENTS.

ELL, be sure! who ever saw such a lad ! Sent out to play at four o' the clock, and all o'er mud at five! Where hast thou been, Will? Speak the truth, now!"

"Been down by the brook rush-plaiting," said little Will, looking as if his mind were not quite made up whether to cry or to be sulky.

"The mischievousness of lads! Didn't I tell thee to mind and keep thy clothes clean?"

"You're always after clothes! How could I plait rushes and keep 'em clean?"

"And who told you to plait rushes, Master Impudence? Take that." *That* was a sound box on the ear which Ursula delivered by way of illustration to her remarks. "What's become o' Phil Tye? I thought he was going to look after thee."

"Well, he did, a bit: then he and Jem Morris went off bird-nesting."

"I'll give it him when I see him! Where's Cicely?"

"She's somewhere," said Will, looking round the cottage, as if he expected to see her in some corner.

"I reckon I could have told thee so much. Did Mistress Wade find you?"

"She was down at the brook: but she went after Cis."

"Well, thou'lt have to go to bed first thing, for them clothes must be washed."

Will broke into a howl. "It isn't bed-time nor it isn't washing-day!"

"It's bed-time when thou'rt bidden to go. As to washing-day, it's always washing-day where thou art. Never was such a boy, I do believe, for getting into the mud. Thou'rt worser ten times o'er than thou wert. I do wish lads 'd stop babes till they're men, that one could tuck 'em in the cradle and leave 'em! There's never a bit of peace! I would the Black Ladies 'd come for you. I shall be mighty thankful when they do, be sure."

"Mistress Wade 'll have us," suggested Master William, briskly, looking up at Ursula.

"Hold that pert tongue o' thine! Mistress Wade's not like to have you. You're in my care, and I've no leave to deliver you to any save the Black Ladies."

"Well! I wouldn't mind camping out a bit, if you're so set to be rid of us," said Will, reflectively. "There's a blanket you've got rolled up in the loft, that 'd make a tent, and we could cut down poles, if you'll lend us an axe; and——"

"You cut down poles! Marry come up! You're not about to have any of my blankets, nor my axes neither."

"It wouldn't be so bad," Will went on, still in a meditative key, "only for dinner. I don't see where we should get that."

"I see that you're off to bed this minute, and don't go maundering about tents and axes. You cut down poles! you'd cut your fingers off, more like. Now then, be off to the loft! Not another word! March!"

Just as Ursula was sweeping Will up-stairs before her, a rap came on the door.

"There! didn't I say a body never had a bit of peace?—Go on, Will, and get to bed; and mind thou leaves them dirty clothes on the floor by theirselves:

don't go to dirt everything in the room with 'em.—
Walk in, Mistress Wade! So you found Cis?"

"Ay, I found her," said the landlady, as she and
Cissy came in together.

"Cis, do thou go up, maid, and see to Will a bit.
He's come in all o'er mud and mire, and I sent him up
to bed, but there's no trusting him to go. See he does,
prithee, and cast his clothes into the tub yonder, there's
a good maid."

Cissy knew very well that Ursula spoke so amiably
because Mrs. Wade was there to hear her. She went
up to look after her little brother, and the landlady
turned to Ursula.

"Now, Ursula Felstede, I want these children."

"Then you must ask leave from the Queen's Commissioners, Mistress Wade. Eh, I couldn't give 'em up if
it were ever so! I daren't, for the life o' me!"

Mrs. Wade begged, coaxed, lectured, and almost
threatened her, but for once Ursula was firm. She
dared not give up the children, and she was quite honest
in saying so. Mrs. Wade had to go home without
them.

As she came up, very weary and unusually dispirited,
to the archway of the King's Head, she heard voices
from within.

"I tell you she's not!" said Dorothy Denny's voice
in a rather frightened tone; "she went forth nigh four
hours agone, and whither I know not."

"That's an inquiry for me," said Mrs. Wade to herself, as she sprang down from her old black mare, and
gave her a pat before dismissing her to the care of the
ostler, who ran up to take her. "Good Jenny! good
old lass!—Is there any company, Giles?" she asked of
the ostler.

"Mistress, 'tis Master Maynard the Sheriff, and he's

making inquiration for you. I would you could ha' kept away a bit longer!"

"Dost thou so, good Giles? Well, I would as God would. The Sheriff had best have somebody else to deal with him than Doll and Bab." And she went forward into the kitchen.

Barbara, her younger servant, who was only a girl, stood leaning against a dresser, looking very white and frightened, with the rolling-pin in her hand; she had evidently been stopped in the middle of making a pie. Dorothy stood on the hearth, fronting the terrible Sheriff, who was armed with a writ, and evidently did not mean to leave before he had seen the mistress.

"I am here, Mr. Maynard, if you want me," said Mrs. Wade, quite calmly.

"Well said," answered the Sheriff, turning to her. "I have here a writ for your arrest, my mistress, and conveyance to the Bishop's Court at London, there to answer for your ill deeds."

"I am ready to answer for all my deeds, good and ill, to any that have a right to question me. I will go with you.—Bab, go and tell Giles to leave the saddle on Jenny.—Doll, here be my keys; take them, and do the best thou canst. I believe thee honest and well-meaning, but I'm feared the house shall ne'er keep up its credit. Howbeit, that cannot be helped. Do thy best, and the Lord be with you! As to directions, I were best to leave none; maybe they should but hamper thee, and set thee in perplexity. Keep matters clean, and pay as thou goest—thou wist where to find the till; and fear God—that's all I need say. And if it come in thy way to do a kind deed for any, and in especial those poor little children that thou wist of, do it, as I would were I here: ay, and let Cissy know when all's o'er with her father. And pray for me, and I'll do as much

for thee—that we may do our duty and please God, and
for bodily safety let it be according to His will.—Now,
Master Maynard, I am ready."

Four days later, several strokes were rung on the great
bell of the Bishop's Palace at Fulham. The gaoler
came to his gate when summoned by the porter.

"Here's a prisoner up from Colchester—Philippa
Wade, hostess of the King's Head there. Have you
room ?"

"Room and to spare. Heresy, I reckon ?"

"Ay, heresy,—the old tale. There must be a nest of
it yonder down in Essex."

"There's nought else all o'er the country, methinks,"
said the gaoler with a laugh. "Come in, Mistress; I'll
show you your lodging. His Lordship hath an apartment in especial, furnished of polished black oak, that
he keepeth for such as you. Pray you follow me."

Mrs. Wade followed the jocose gaoler along a small
paved passage between two walls, and through a low
door, which the gaoler barred behind her, himself outside,
and then opened a little wicket through which to speak.

"Pray you, sit down, my mistress, on whichsoever of
the chairs you count desirable. The furniture is all of
one sort, fair and goodly ; far-fetched and dear-bought,
which is good for gentlewomen, and liketh them : fast
colours the broidery, I do ensure you."

Mrs. Wade looked round, so far as she could see by
the little wicket, everything was black—even the floor,
which was covered with black shining lumps of all
shapes and sizes. She touched one of the lumps. There
could be no doubt of its nature. The "polished black
oak" furniture was cobs of coal, and the sumptuous
apartment wherein she was to be lodged was Bishop
Bonner's coal-cellar.

CHAPTER XXXII.

"READY! AYE, READY!"

IT was the evening of the first of August. The prisoners in the Castle, now reduced to four—the Mounts, Rose, and Johnson —had held their Bible-reading and their little evening prayer-meeting, and sat waiting for supper. John and Margaret Thurston, who had been with them until that day, were taken away in the morning to undergo examination, and had not returned. The prisoners had not yet heard when they were to die. They only knew that it would be soon, and might be any day. Yet we are told they remained in their dungeons "with much joy and great comfort, in continual reading and invocating the name of God, ever looking and expecting the happy day of their dissolution."

We should probably feel more inclined to call it a horrible day. But they called it a happy day. They expected to change their prison for a palace, and their prison bonds for golden harps, and the prison fare for the fruit of the Tree of Life, and the company of scoffers and tormentors for that of Seraphim and Cherubim, and the blessed dead: and above all, to see His Face who had laid down His life for them.

Supper was late that evening. They could hear voices outside, with occasional exclamations of surprise, and now and then a peal of laughter. At length the door was unlocked, and the gaoler's man came in with four trenchers, piled on each other, on each of which was laid a slice of rye-bread and a piece of cheese. He served out one to each prisoner.

"Want your appetites sharpened?" said he with a sarcastic laugh. "Because, if you do, there's news for you."

"Prithee let us hear it, Bartle," answered Mount, quietly.

"Well, first, writs is come down. Moot Hall prisoners suffer at six to-morrow, on the waste by Lexden Road, and you'll get your deserving i' th' afternoon, in the Castle yard."

"God be praised!" solemnly responded William Mount, and the others added an Amen.

"Well, you're a queer set!" said Bartle, looking at them. "I shouldn't want to thank nobody for it, if so be I was going to be hanged : and that's easier of the two."

"We are only going Home," answered William Mount. "The climb may be steep, but there is rest and ease at the end thereof."

"Well, you seem mighty sure on't. I know nought. Priests say you'll find yourselves in a worser place nor you think."

"Nay! God is faithful," said Johnson.

"Have it your own way. I wish you might, for you seem to me a deal tidier folks than most that come our way. Howbeit, my news isn't all told. Alegar, your brats be gone to Hedingham."

"God go with them!" replied Johnson; but he seemed much sadder to hear this than he had done for his own doom.

"And Margaret Thurston's recanted. She's reconciled and had to better lodging."

It was evident, though to Bartle's astonishment, that the prisoners considered this the worst news of all.

"And John Thurston?"

"Ah, they aren't so sure of him. They think he'll cear a faggot, but it's not certain yet."

"God help and strengthen him!"

"And Mistress Wade, of the King's Head, is had up to London to the Bishop."

"God grant her His grace!"

"I've told you all now. Good-night."

The greeting was returned, and Bartle went out. He was commissioned to carry the writ down to the Moot Hall.

Not many minutes later, Wastborowe entered the dungeon with the writ in his hand. The prisoners were conversing over their supper, but the sight of that document brought silence without any need to call for it.

"Hearken!" said Wastborowe. "At six o'clock in the morning, on the waste piece by Lexden Road, shall suffer the penalty of the law these men and women underwritten:— William Bongeor, Thomas Benold, Robert *alias* William Purcas, Agnes Silverside *alias* Downes *alias* Smith *alias* May, Helen Ewring, Elizabeth Foulkes, Agnes Bowyer."

With one accord, led by Mr. Benold, the condemned prisoners stood up and thanked God.

"'Agnes Bowyer,'" repeated Wastborowe in some perplexity. "Your name's not Bowyer; it's Bongeor."

"Bongeor," said its bearer. "Is my name wrong set down? Pray you, Mr. Wastborowe, have it put right without delay, that I be not left out."

"I should think you'd be uncommon glad if you were!" said he.

"Nay, but in very deed it should grieve me right

sore," she replied earnestly. "Let there not be no mistake, I do entreat you."

"I'll see to it," said Wastborowe, as he left the prison.

The prisoners had few preparations to make. Each had a garment ready—a long robe of white linen, falling straight from the neck to the ankles, with sleeves which buttoned at the wrist. There were many such robes made during the reign of Mary—types of those fairer white robes which would be "given to every one of them," when they should have crossed the dark valley, and come out into the light of the glory of God. Only Agnes Bongeor and Helen Ewring had something else to part with. With Agnes in her prison was a little baby only a few weeks old, and she must bid it good-bye, and commit it to the care of some friend. Helen Ewring had to say farewell to her husband, who came to see her about four in the morning ; and to the surprise of Elizabeth Foulkes, she found herself summoned also to an interview with her widowed mother and her uncle Holt.

"Why, Mother!" exclaimed Elizabeth in astonishment, "I never knew you were any where nigh."

"Didst thou think, my lass, that aught 'd keep thy mother away from thee when she knew? I've been here these six weeks, a-waiting to hear. Eh, my pretty mawther,[1] but to see this day ! I've looked for thee to be some good man's wife, and a happy woman,—such a good maid as thou always wast !—and now! Well, well ! the will of the Lord be done ! "

"A happy woman, Mother!" said Elizabeth with her brightest smile. "In all my life I never was so happy as this day ! This is my wedding day—nay, this is my crowning day ! For ere the sun be high this day, I

---

[1] Girl. This is a Suffolk provincialism.

shall have seen the Face of Christ, and have been by Him presented faultless before the light of the glory of God. Mother, rejoice with me, and rejoice for me, for I can do nothing save rejoice. Glory be to God on high, and on earth peace, good-will towards men!"

There was glory to God, but little good-will towards men, when the six prisoners were marched out into High Street, on their way to martyrdom. Yet only one sorrowful heart was in the dungeon of the Moot Hall, and that was Agnes Bongeor's, who lamented bitterly that owing to the mis-spelling of her name in the writ, she was not allowed to make the seventh. She actually put on her robe of martyrdom, in the *hope* that she might be reckoned among the sufferers. Now, when she learned that she was not to be burned that day, her distress was poignant.

"Let me go with them!" she cried. "Let me go and give my life for Christ! Alack the day! The Lord counts me not worthy."

The other six prisoners were led, tied together, two and two, through High Street and up to the Head Gate. First came William Bongeor and Thomas Benold; then Mrs. Silverside and Mrs. Ewring; last, Robert Purcas and Elizabeth Foulkes. They were led out of the Head Gate, to "a plot of ground hard by the town wall, on the outward side," beside the Lexden Road. There stood three great wooden stakes, with a chain affixed to each. The clock of St. Mary-at-Walls struck six as they reached the spot.

Around the stakes a multitude were gathered to see the sight. Mr. Ewring, with set face, trying to force a smile for his wife's encouragement; Mrs. Foulkes, gazing with clasped hands and tearful eyes on her daughter; Thomas Holt and all his family; Mr. Ashby and all his; Ursula Felstede, looking very unhappy; Dorothy

Denny, looking very sad; old Walter Purcas, leaning
on his staff, from time to time shaking his white head as
if in bitter lamentation; a little behind the others, Mrs.
Clere and Amy; and in front, busiest of the busy, Sir
Thomas Tye and Nicholas Clere.   There they all were,
ready and waiting, to see the Moot Hall prisoners die.

CHAPTER XXXIII.

HOW THEY WENT HOME.

RRIVED at the spot where they were to suffer, the prisoners knelt down to pray: "but not in such sort as they would, for the cruel tyrants would not suffer them." Foremost of their tormentors at this last moment was Nicholas Clere, who showed an especial spite towards Elizabeth Foulkes, and interrupted her dying prayers to the utmost of his power. When Elizabeth rose from her knees and took off her outer garments—underneath which she wore the prepared robe—she asked the Bailiff's leave to give her petticoat to her mother; it was all the legacy in her power to leave. Even this poor little comfort was denied her. The clothes of the sufferers were the perquisite of the Sheriffs' men, and they would not give them up. Elizabeth smiled—she did nothing but smile that morning—and cast the petticoat on the ground.

"Farewell, all the world!" she said. "Farewell, Faith! farewell, Hope!" Then she took the stake in her arms and kissed it. "Welcome, Love!"

Ay, faith and hope were done with now. A few moments, and faith would be lost in sight; hope would be lost in joy; but love would abide for ever and ever.

Her mother came up and kissed her.

"My blessed dear," she said, "be strong in the Lord!"

They chained the two elder men at one stake; the two women at another : Elizabeth and Robert together at the last. The Sheriffs' men put the chain round them both, and hammered the other end fast, so that they should not attempt to escape.

Escape! none of them dreamed of such a thing. They cared neither for pain nor shame. To their eyes Heaven itself was open, and the Lord Christ, on the right hand of the Father, would rise to receive His servants. Nor did they say much to each other. There would be time for that when all was over ! Were they not going the journey together? would they not dwell in happy company, through the long years of eternity?

The man who was nailing the chain close to where Elizabeth stood accidentally let his hammer slip. He had not intended to hurt her; but the hammer came down heavily upon her shoulder and made a severe wound. She turned her head to him and smiled on him. Then she lifted up her eyes to heaven and prayed. Her last few moments were spent in alternate prayer and exhortation of the crowd.

The torch was applied to the firewood and tar-barrels heaped around them. As the flame sprang up, the six martyrs clapped their hands : and from the bystanders a great cry rose to heaven,—

"The Lord strengthen them! the Lord comfort them! the Lord pour His mercies upon them !"

Ah, it was not England, but Rome, who burned those Marian martyrs ! The heart of England was sound and true ; she was a victim, not a persecutor.

Just as the flame reached its fiercest heat, there was a slight cry in the crowd, which parted hither and thither as a girl was borne out of it insensible. She had fainted after uttering that cry. It was no wonder said those who stood near : the combined heat of the

August sun and the fire was scarcely bearable. She would come round shortly if she were taken into the shade to recover.

Half-an-hour afterwards nothing could be seen beside the Lexden Road but the heated and twisted chains, with fragments of charred wood and of grey ashes. The crowd had gone home.

And the martyrs had gone home too. No more should the sun light upon them, nor any heat. The Lamb in the midst of the Throne had led them to living fountains of water, and they were comforted for evermore.

" Who was that young woman that swooned and had to be borne away ? " asked a woman in the crowd of another, as they made their way back into the town.

The woman appealed to was Audrey Wastborowe.

"Oh, it was Amy Clere of the Magpie," said she. " The heat was too much for her, I reckon."

" Ay, it was downright hot," said the neighbour.

Something beside the heat had been too much for Amy Clere. The familiar face of Elizabeth Foulkes, with that unearthly smile upon it, had gone right to the girl's heart. For Amy had a heart, though it had been overlaid by a good deal of rubbish.

The crowd did not disperse far. They were gathered again in the afternoon in the Castle yard, when the Mounts and Johnson and Rose Allen were brought out to die. They came as joyfully as their friends had done, " calling upon the name of God, and exhorting the people earnestly to flee from idolatry." Once more the cry rose up from the whole crowd,—

" Lord, strengthen them, and comfort them, and pour Thy mercy upon them ! "

And the Lord heard and answered. Joyfully, joyfully they went home, and the happy company who had stood true, and had been faithful unto death, were all gathered together for ever in the starry halls above.

To two other places the cry penetrated: to Agnes Bongeor weeping in the Moot Hall because she was shut out from that blessed company; and to Margaret Thurston in her "better lodging" in the Castle, who had shut herself out, and had bought life by the denial of her Lord.

The time is not far off when we too shall be asked to choose between these two alternatives. Not, perhaps, between earthly life and death (though it may come to that): but between faith and unfaithfulness, between Christ and idols, between the love that will give up all and the self-love that will endure nothing. Which shall it be with you? Will you add your voice to the side which tamely yields the priceless treasures purchased for us by these noble men and women at this awful cost? or will you meet the Romanising enemy with a firm front, and a shout of "No fellowship with idols!— no surrender of the liberty which our fathers bought with their heart's blood!" God grant you grace to choose the last!

When Mrs. Clere reached the Magpie, she went up to Amy's room, and found her lying on the bed with her face turned to the wall.

"Amy! what ailed thee, my maid?—art better now?"

"Mother, we're all wrong!"

"Dear heart, what does the child mean?" inquired the puzzled mother. "Has the sun turned thy wits out o' door?"

"The sun did nought to me, mother. It was Bessie's face that I could not bear. Bessie's face, that I knew so well—the face that had lain beside me on this pillow over and over again—and that smile upon her lips, as if she were half in Heaven already—Mother it was dreadful! I felt as if the last day were come, and the angels were shutting me out."

"Hush thee, child, hush thee! 'Tis not safe to speak such things. Heretics go to the ill place, as thou very well wist."

"Names don't matter, do they, Mother? It is truth that signifies. Whatever names they please to call Bessie Foulkes, she had Heaven and not Hell in her face. That smile of hers never came from Satan. I know what his smiles are like: I've seen them on other faces afore now. He never had nought to do with her."

"Amy, if thy father hears thee say such words as those, he'll be proper angry, be sure!"

Amy sat up on the bed.

"Mother, you know that Bessie Foulkes loved God, and feared Him, and cared to please Him, as you and I never did in all our lives. Do folks that love God go to Satan? Does He punish people because they want to please Him? I know little enough about it, alack-the-day! but if an angel came from Heaven to tell me Bessie wasn't there this minute, I could not believe him."

"Well, well! think what you will, child, only don't say it! I've nothing against Bess being in Heaven, not I! I hope she may be, poor lass. But thou knowest thy father's right set against it all, and the priests too; and, Amy, I don't want to see *thee* on the waste by Lexden Road. Just hold thy tongue, wilt thou? or thou'lt find thyself in the wrong box afore long."

"Mother, I don't think Bessie Foulkes is sorry for what happened this morning."

"Maybe not, but do hold thy peace!"

"I can hold my peace if you bid me, Mother. I've not been a good girl, but I mean to try and be better. I don't feel as if I should ever care again for the gewgaws and the merrymakings that I used to think all the world of. It's like as if I'd had a glimpse into Heaven as she went in, and the world had lost its savour. But don't be feared, Mother; I'll not vex you, nor Father neither, if you don't wish me to talk. Only—nobody'll keep me from trying to go after Bessie!"

CHAPTER XXXIV

DOROTHY TAKES A MESSAGE.

OW then, attend, can't you? How much sugar?"

"Please, Sister Mary, my head does ache so!"

"No excuses, Cicely! Answer at once."

A long sobbing sigh preceded the words—"Half a pound."

"Now get to your sewing. Cicely, I must be obeyed; and your are a right perverse child as one might look for with the training you have had. Let me hear no more about headache: it's nothing but nonsense."

"But my head does ache dreadfully, Sister."

"Well, it is your own fault, if it do. Two mortal hours were you crying last night,—the stars know what for!"

"It was because I didn't hear nothing about Father," said poor Cissy sorrowfully. "Mistress Wade promised she——"

"Mistress Wade—who is that?"

"Please, she's the hostess of the King's Head: and she said she would let me know when——"

"When what?"

"When Father couldn't have any pain ever any more."

"Do you mean that you wish to hear your Father is dead, you wicked child?"

Cissy looked up wearily into the nun's face. "He's in pain now," she said; "for he is waiting, and knows he will have more. But when it has come, he will have no more, never, but will live with God and be happy for ever and ever. I want to know that Father's happy."

"How can these wicked heretics fall into such delusions?" said Sister Mary, looking across the room at Sister Joan, who shook her head in a way which seemed to say that there was no setting any bounds to the delusions of heretics. "Foolish child, thy father is a bad man, and bad men do not go to Heaven."

"Father's not a bad man," said Cissy, not angrily, but in a tone of calm persuasion that nothing would shake. "I cry you mercy, Sister Mary, but you don't know him, and somebody has told you wrong. Father's good, and loves God; and people are not bad when they love God and do what He says to them. You're mistaken, please, Sister."

"But thy father does not obey God, child, because he does not obey the Church."

"Please, I don't know anything about the Church. Father obeys the Bible, and that is God's own Word which He spoke Himself. The Church can't be any better than that."

"The Church, for thee, is the priest, who will tell thee how to please God and the Holy Mother, if thou wilt hearken."

"But the priest's a man, Sister: and God's Book is a great deal better than that."

"The priest is in God's stead, and conveys His commands."

"But I've got the commands, Sister Mary, in the Book; and God hasn't written a new one, has He?"

"Silly child! the Church is above any Book."

"Oh no, it can't be, Sister, please. What Father bade me do his own self must be better than what other people bid me; and so what God says in His own Book must be better than what other people say, and the Church is only people."

"Cicely, be silent! Thou art a very silly, perverse child."

"I dare say I am, Sister, but I am sure that's true."

Sister Joan was on the point of bidding Cissy hold her tongue in a still more authoritative manner, when one of the lay Sisters entered the room, to say that a woman asked permission to speak with one of the teaching Sisters.

"What is her name?"

"She says her name is Denny."

"Denny! I know nobody of that name."

"Oh, please, is her name Dorothy?" asked Cissy, eagerly. "If it's Dorothy Denny, Mrs. Wade has sent her—she's Mrs. Wade's servant. Oh, do let me——"

"Silence!" said Sister Mary. "I will go and speak with the woman."

She found in the guest-chamber a woman of about thirty, who stood dropping courtesies as if she were very uncomfortable.

Very uncomfortable Dorothy Denny was. She did not know what "nervous" meant, but she was exceedingly nervous for all that. In the first place, she felt extremely doubtful whether if she trusted herself inside a convent, she would ever have a chance of getting out again; and in the second she was deeply concerned about several things, of which one was Cissy.

" What do you want, good woman ? "

" Please you, Madam, I cry you mercy for troubling of you, but if I might speak a word with the dear child——"

" What dear child ? " asked the nun placidly.

Dorothy's fright grew. Were they going to deny Cissy to her, or even to say that she was not there ?

" Please you, good Sister, I mean little Cis—Cicely Johnson, an' it like you, that I was sent to with a message from my mistress, the hostess of the King's Head in Colchester."

" Cicely Johnson is not now at liberty. You can give the message to me."

" May I wait till I can see her ? "

Plainly, Dorothy was no unfaithful messenger when her own comfort only was to be sacrificed. Sister Mary considered a moment ; and then said she would see if Cicely could be allowed to have an interview with her visitor. Bidding Dorothy sit down, she left the room.

For quite an hour Dorothy sat waiting, until she began to think the nuns must have forgotten her existence, and to look about for some means of reminding them of it. There were no bells in sitting-rooms at that time, except in the form of a little hand-bell on a table, and for this last Dorothy searched in vain. Then she tried to go out into the passage, in the hope of seeing somebody ; but she was terrified to find herself locked in. She did not know what to do. The window was barred with an iron grating ; there was no escape that way. Poor Dorothy began to wonder whether, if she found herself a prisoner, she could contrive to climb the chimney, and what would become of her after doing so, when she heard at last the welcome sound of approaching steps, and the key was turned in

N

the lock. The next minute Cissy was in Dorothy's arms.

"O Dorothy! dear Dorothy! tell me quick—Father——" Cissy could get no further.

"He is at rest, my dear heart, and shall die no more."

Cissy was not able to answer for the sobs that choked her voice, and Dorothy smoothed her hair and petted her.

"Nay, grieve not thus, sweet heart," she said.

"Oh no, it is so wicked of me!" sobbed poor Cissy. "I thought I should have been so glad for Father: and I can only think of me and the children. We've got no father now!"

"Nay, my dear heart, thou hast as much as ever thou hadst. He is only gone upstairs and left you down. He isn't dead, little Cissy: he's alive in a way he never was before, and he shall live for ever and ever."

Neither Dorothy nor Cissy had noticed that a nun had entered with her, and they were rather startled to hear a voice out of the dark corner by the door.

"Take heed, good woman, how thou learn the child such errors. That is only true of great saints; and the man of whom you speak was a wicked heretic."

"I know not what sort of folks your saints are," said Dorothy bravely: "but my saints are folks that love God and desire to please Him, and that John Johnson was, if ever a man were in this evil world. An evil tree cannot bring forth good fruit."

The nun crossed herself, but she did not answer.

"It would be as well if folks would be content to set the bad folks in prison, and let the good ones be," said Dorothy. "Cissy, our mistress is up to London to the Bishop."

" Will they do somewhat to her ? "

" God knoweth ! " said Dorothy, shaking her head sorrowfully. "I shall be fain if I may see her back ; oh, I shall ! "

" Oh, I hope they won't ! " said Cissy, her eyes filling again with tears. "I love Mistress Wade."

CHAPTER XXXV.

NOBODY LEFT FOR CISSY.

PLEASE, Dorothy, what's become of Rose Allen ? and Bessy Foulkes ? and Mistress Mount, and all of them ?"

"All gone, my dear heart—all with thy father."

"Are they all gone ?" said Cissy with another sob. "Isn't there one left ?"

"Not one of them."

"Then if we came out, we shouldn't find nobody ?"

"Prithee reckon not, Cicely," said the nun, "that thou art likely to come out. There is no such likelihood at all whilst our good Queen reigneth ; and if it please God, she shall have a son after her that shall be true to the Catholic faith, as she is, and not suffer evil courses and naughty heretics to be any more in the realm. Ye will abide here till it be plainly seen whether God shall grant to thee and thy sister the grace of a vocation; and if not, it shall be well seen to that ye be in care of good Catholic folk, that shall look to it ye go in the right way. So prithee, suffer not thy fancy to deceive thee with any thought of going forth of this house of religion When matters be somewhat better established, and the lands whereof the Church hath been robbed are given back to her, and all the religious put back in their houses, or new ones built, then will England be an Isle of Saints as in olden time, and men may rejoice thereat."

Cissy listened to this long speech, which she only understood in part, but she gathered that the nuns meant to keep her a prisoner as long as they could.

"But Sister Joan," said she, "you don't know, do you, what God is going to do? Perhaps he will give us another good king or queen, like King Edward. I ask Him to do, every day. But, please, what is a vocation?"

"Thou dost, thou wicked maid? I never heard thee."

"But I don't ask you, Sister Joan. I ask God. And I think He'll do it, too. What is a vocation, please?"

"What I'm afeared thou wilt never have, thou sinful heretic child—the call to become a holy Sister."

"Who is to call me? I am a sister now; I'm Will's and Baby's sister. Nobody can't call me to be a sister to nobody else," said Cissy, getting very negative in her earnestness.

Sister Joan rose from her seat. "The time is up," said she. "Say farewell to thy friend."

"Farewell, Dorothy dear," said Cissy, clinging to the one person she knew, who seemed to belong to her past, as she never would have thought of doing to Dorothy Denny in bygone days. "Please give Mistress Wade my duty, when she comes home, and say I'm trying to do as Father bade me, and I'll never, never believe nothing he told me not. You see they couldn't do nothing to me save burn me, as they did Father, and then I should go to Father, and all would be right directly. It's much better for them all that they are safe there, and I'll try to be glad—thought here's nobody left for me. Father'll have company: I must try and think of that. I thought he'd find nobody he knew but Mother, but if they've all gone too, there'll be plenty. And I suppose there'll be some holy angels to look after us, because God isn't gone away, you see: He's there and here too. He'll help me still to look after Will and

Baby, now I haven't—" a sob interrupted the words—
"haven't got Father. Good-bye, Dolly! Kiss me,
please. Nobody never kisses me now."

"Thou poor little dear !" cried Dorothy, fairly melted,
and sobbing over Cissy as she gave her half-a-dozen
kisses at least. "The Lord bless thee, and be good to
thee! I'm sure He'll take proper vengeance on every
body as isn't. I wouldn't like to be them as ill-used
thee. They'll have a proper bill to pay in the next
world, if they don't get it in this. Poor little pretty
dear !"

"You will drink a cup of ale and eat a manchet ?"
asked Sister Joan of Dorothy.

A manchet was a cake of the best bread.

"No, I thank you, Sister, I am not a-hungered," was
the answer.

"But, Dolly, you did not come all the way from Colchester ?" said Cissy.

"Ay, I did so, my dear, in the miller's cart, and I'm
journeying back in the same. I covenanted to meet
him down at the end of yonder lane at three o'clock,
and methinks I had best be on my way."

"Ay, you have no time to lose," responded Sister
Joan.

Dorothy found Mr. Ewring waiting for her at the end
of the lane.

"Have you had to eat, Dorothy ?" was his first
question when she had climbed up beside him.

"Never a bite or sup in *that* house, Master, I thank
you," was Dorothy's rejoinder. "If I'd been starving
o' hunger, I wouldn't have touched a thing."

"Have you seen the children ?"

"I've seen Cissy. That was enough and to spare."

"What do they with her ?"

"They are working hard with both hands to make an

angel of her at the soonest—that's what they are doing.
It's not what they mean to do. They want to make her
a devil, or one of the devil's children, which comes to
the same thing: but the Lord 'll not suffer that, or I'm
a mistaken woman. They are trying to bend her, and
they never will. She'll break first. So they'll break
her, and then there'll be no more they can do. That's
about where it is, Master Ewring."

"Why, Dorothy, I never saw you thus stirred aforetime."

"Maybe not. It takes a bit to stir me, but I've got
it this even, I can tell you."

"I could well-nigh mistake you for Mistress Wade,"
said Mr. Ewring with a smile.

"Eh, poor Mistress! but if she could see that poor
little dear, it would grieve her to her heart. Master
Ewring, how long will the Lord bear with these sons of
Satan !"

"Ah, Dorothy, that's more than you or I can tell.
'Many shall be purified, and made white, and tried':
that is all we know."

"How much is many?" asked Dorothy almost bitterly.

"Not one too many," said the miller gravely: "and
not one too few. We are called to wait until our
brethren be accomplished that shall suffer. It may be
shorter than we think. But, Dorothy, who set you
among the prophets? I rather thought you had not
over much care for such things."

"Master Ewring, I've heard say that when a soldier's
killed in battle, another steppeth up behind without
delay to fill his place. There's some places wants filling
at Colchester, where the firing's been fierce of late: and
when most of the old warriors be killed, they'll be like
to fill the ranks up with new recruits. And if they be
a bit awkward, and don't step just up to pace, maybe

they'll learn by and by, and meantime the others must have patience."

"The Lord perfect that which concerneth thee!" said the miller, with much feeling. "Dorothy, was your mistress not desirous to have brought up these little ones herself?"

"She was so, Master Ewring, and I would with all my heart she could. Poor little dears!"

"I would have taken the lad, if it might have been compassed, when he was a bit older, and have bred him up to my own trade. The maids should have done better with good Mistress Wade."

"Eh, Master, little Cicely's like to dwell in other 'keeping than either, and that's with her good father and mother above."

"The Lord's will be done!" responded Mr. Ewring. If so be, she at least will have little sorrow."

CHAPTER XXXVI

INTO THE LION'S MOUTH.

IVE you good den, Master Hiltoft! May a man have speech of your prisoner, Mistress Bongeor?"

"You're a bold man, Master Ewring."

"Wherefore?"

"Wherefore! Setting your head in the lion's mouth! I should have thought you'd keep as far from Moot Hall as you could compass. Yourself not unsuspected, and had one burned already from your house—I marvel at you that you hide not yourself behind your corn-measures and flour-sacks, and have a care not to show your face in the street. And here up you march as bold as Hector, and desire to have speech of a prisoner! Well—it's your business, not mine."

"Friend, mine hearth is desolate, and I have only God to my friend. Do you marvel that I haste to do His work whilst it is day, or that I desire to be approved of Him?"

"You go a queer way about it. I reckon you think with the old saw,[1] 'The nearer the church the further from Heaven'?"

"That is true but in some sense. Verily, the nearer some churches, and some priests, so it is. May I see Mistress Bongeor?"

---

[1] Proverb.

" Ay, you would fain not commit yourself, I see, more
than may be. Come, you have a bit of prudence left.
So much the better for you. Come in, and I'll see if
Wastborowe's in a reasonable temper, and that hangs
somewhat on the one that Audrey's in."

The porter shut the gate behind Mr. Ewring, and
went to seek Wastborowe. Just then Jane Hiltoft,
coming to her door, saw him waiting, and invited him
to take a seat.

" Fine morning, Master."

" Ay, it is, Jane. Have you yet here poor Johnson's
little maid ? "

" I haven't, Master, and I feel fair lost without the
dear babe. A rare good child she was—never see a
better. The Black Ladies of Hedingham has got her,
and I'm all to pieces afeard they'll not tend her right
way. How should nuns (saving their holy presences)
know aught about babes and such like? Eh dear!
they'd better have left her with me. I'd have taken to
her altogether, if Simon'd have let me—and I think
he would after a bit. And she'd have done well with
me, too."

" Ay, Jane, you'd have cared her well for the body,
I cast no doubt."

" Dear heart, but it's sore pity, Master Ewring, such
a good man as you cannot be a good Catholic like everybody else ! You'd save yourself ever so much trouble
and sorrow. I cannot think why you don't."

" We should save ourselves a little sorrow, Jane; but
we should have a deal more than we lost."

" But how so, Master ?   It's only giving up an
opinion."

" Maybe so, with some : but not with us. They that
have been taught this way by others, and never knew
Christ for themselves—with them, as you say, it were

but the yielding of opinion : but to us that know Him, and have heard His voice, it would be the betraying of the best Friend in earth or Heaven. And we cannot do that, Jane Hiltoft—not even for life."

"Nay, that stands to reason if it were so, Master Ewring; but, trust me, I know not what you mean, no more than if you spake Latin."

"Read God's Book, and pray for His Spirit, and you shall find out, Jane.—Well, Hiltoft ? "

"Wastborowe says you may see Mistress Bongeor if you'll give him a royal farthing, but he won't let you for a penny less. He's had words with their Audrey, and he's as savage as Denis of Siccarus."

"Who was he, Hiltoft ? " answered Mr. Ewring with a smile, as he felt in his purse for the half-crown which was to be the price of his visit to Agnes Bongeor.

"Eh, I don't know: I heard Master Doctor say the other day that his dog was as fierce as him."

"Art sure he said not ' Syracuse ' ? "

"Dare say he might. Syracuse or Siccarus, all's one to me."

At the door of the dungeon stood the redoubtable Wastborowe, his keys hanging from his girdle, and looking, to put it mildly, not particularly amiable.

"Want letting out again by and by ? " he inquired with grim satire, as Mr. Ewring put the coin in his hand.

"If you please, Wastborowe. You've no writ to keep me, have you ? "

"Haven't—worse luck ! Only wish I had. I'd set a match to the lot of you with as much pleasure as I'd drink a pot of ale. It'll never be good world till we're rid of heretics ! "

"There'll be Satan left then, methinks, and maybe a few rogues and murderers to boot."

"Never a one as bad as you Lutherans and Gospellers! Get you in. You'll have to wait my time to
come out."

"Very well," said Mr. Ewring quietly, and went in.

He found Agnes Bongeor seated in a corner of the
window recess, with her Bible on her knee; but it was
closed, and she looked very miserable.

"Well, my sister, and how is it with you?"

"As 'tis like to be, Master Ewring, with her whom
the Lord hath cast forth, and reckons unworthy to do
Him a service."

"Did he so reckon Abraham, then, at the time of the
offering up of Isaac? Isaac was not sacrificed: he was
turned back from the same. Yet what saith the Lord
unto him? 'Because thou hast done this thing, and
hast not withheld thy son, thou shalt be blessed, because
thou hast obeyed My voice.' See you, his good will
thereto is reckoned as though he had done the thing.
'The Lord looketh on the heart.' Doubt thou not, my
good sister, but firmly believe, that to thee also faith is
counted for righteousness, and the will passeth for the
deed, with Him who saith that 'if thou be Christ's then
art thou Abraham's seed.'"

"That's comforting, in truth," said poor Agnes.
"But, Master Ewring, think you there is any hope that
I may yet be allowed to witness for my Lord before men
in very deed? To have come so near, and be thrust
back! Is there no hope?"

Agnes Bongeor was not the only one of the sufferers
in this persecution who actually coveted and longed for
martyrdom. If the imperial crown of all the world
had been laid at their feet, they would have reckoned
it beneath contempt in comparison with that crown of
life promised to such as are faithful unto death. Not
faithful *till* death, but *unto* it.

" I know not what the Lord holds in reserve for thee, my sister. I only know that whatsoever it be, it is that whereby thou mayest best glorify Him. Is that not enough ? If more glory should come to Him by thy dying in this dungeon after fifty years' imprisonment, than by thy burning, which wouldst thou choose ? Speak truly."

Agnes dropped her face upon her hands for a moment.

" You have the right, Master Ewring," said she, when she looked up again. " I fear I was over full of myself. Let the Lord's will be done, and His glory ensured, by His doing with me whatsoever He will. I will strive to be patient, and not grieve more than I should."

" Therein wilt thou do well, my sister. And now ₁ go—whenas it shall please Wastborowe," added Mr. Ewring with a slight smile of amusement, and then growing grave,—" to visit one in far sorer trouble than thyself."

" Eh, Master, who is that ? "

" It is Margaret Thurston, who hath not been, nor counted herself, rejected of the Lord, but hath of her own will rejected Him. She bought life by recanting."

" Eh, poor soul, how miserable must she be ! Tell her, if it like you, that I will pray for her. Maybe the Lord will grant to both of us the grace yet to be His witnesses."

Mr. Ewring had to pass four weary hours in the dungeon before it pleased Wastborowe to let him out. He spent it in conversing with the other prisoners,—all of whom, save Agnes Bongeor, were arrested for some crime,—and trying to do them good. At last the heavy door rolled back, and Wastborowe's voice was heard inquiring, in accents which did not sound particularly sober,—

" Where's yon companion that wants baking by Lexden Road ? "

"I am here, Wastborowe," said Mr. Ewring, rising.
" Good den, friends.   The Lord bless and comfort thee,
my sister ! "

And out he went into the summer evening air, to meet
the half-tipsy gaoler's farewell of,—

" There !   Take to thy heels, old shortbread, afore
thou'rt done a bit too brown.   Thou'lt get it some of
these days ! "

R. EWRING only returned Wastborowe's uncivil farewell by a nod, as he walked up High Street towards East Gate. At the corner of Tenant's Lane he turned to the left, and went up to the Castle. A request to see the prisoner there brought about a little discussion between the porter and the gaoler, and an appeal was apparently made to some higher authority. At length the visitor was informed that permission was granted, on condition that he would not mention the subject of religion.

The condition was rejected at once. Mr. Ewring had come to talk about that and nothing else.

"Then you'd best go home," said Bartle. "Can't do to have matters set a-crooked again when they are but now coming straight. Margaret Thurston's reconciled, and we've hopes for John, though he's been harder of the two to bring round. Never do to have folks coming and setting 'em all wrong side up. Do *you* want to see 'em burned, my master?"

"I want to see them true," was Mr. Ewring's answer. "The burning doesn't much matter."

"Oh, doesn't it?" sneered Bartle. "You'll sing another tune, Master Ewring, the day you're set alight."

" Methinks, friend, those you have burned sang none
other. But how about a thousand years hence ? Bartho-
lomew Crane, what manner of tune wilt thou be singing
then ? "

" Time enough to say when I've got it pricked, Master,"
said Bartle : but Mr. Ewring saw from his uneasiness
that the shot had told.

People were much more musical in England three
hundred years ago than now. Nearly everybody could
sing, or read music at sight : and a lady was thought
very poorly educated if she could not "set "—that is,
write down a tune properly on hearing it played. Writ-
ing music they called " pricking " it.

Mr. Ewring did not stay to talk with Bartle ; he bade
him good-bye, and walked up Tenant's Lane on his way
home. But before he had gone many yards, an idea
struck him, and he turned round and went back to the
Castle.

Bartle was still in the court, and he peeped through
the wicket to see who was there.

" Good lack ! you're come again ! "

" I'm come again," said Mr. Ewring, smiling.
" Bartle, wilt take a message to the Thurstons for
me ? "

" Depends," said Bartle with a knowing nod. " What's
it about ? If you want to tell 'em price of flour, I don't
mind."

" I only want you to say one word to either of them."

" Come, that's jolly ! What's the word ? "

" Remember ! "

Bartle scratched his head. " Remember what ?
There's the rub ! "

" Leave that to them," said Mr. Ewring.

" Well,—I—don't—know," said Bartle very slowly.
" Mayhap *I* sha'n't remember."

" Mayhap that shall help you," replied the miller, holding up an angelet, namely, a gold coin, value 3s. 4d., —the smallest gold coin then made.

" Shouldn't wonder if that strengthened my wits," said Bartle with a grin, as the little piece of gold was slipped through the wicket. " That's over a penny a letter, baint it ? "

" Fivepence. It's good pay."

" It's none so bad. I'm in hopes you'll have a few more messages, Master Ewring. They're easy to carry when they come in a basket o' that metal."

" Ah, Bartle! wilt thou do that for a gold angelet which thou wouldst not for the love of God or thy neighbour ? Beware that all thy good things come not to thee in this life—which can only be if they be things that pertain to this life alone."

" This life's enough for me, Master : it's all I've got."

" Truth, friend. Therefore cast it not away in folly."

" In a good sooth, Master Ewring, I love your angelets better than your preachment, and you paid me not to listen to a sermon, but to carry a message. Good den ! "

" Good den, Bartle. May the Lord give thee good ending ! "

Bartle stood looking from the wicket until the miller had turned the corner.

" Yon's a good man, I do believe," said he to himself. " I marvel what they burn such men for ! They're never found lying or cheating or murdering. Why couldn't folks let 'em alone ? We shouldn't want to hurt 'em, if the priests would let us alone. Marry, this would be a good land if there were no priests ! "

Bartle shut the wicket, and prepared to carry in

supper to his prisoners. John and Margaret Thurston were not together. The priests were afraid to let them be so, lest John, who stood more firmly of the two, should talk over Margaret. They occupied adjoining cells. Bartle opened a little wicket in the first, and called John to receive his rations of brown bread, onions, and weak ale.

"I promised to give you a message," said he, "but I don't know as it's like to do you much good. It's only one word.'

"Should be a weighty one," said John. "What is it?"

"'Remember!'"

"Ah!" John Thurston's long-drawn exclamation, which ended with a heavy sigh, astonished Bartle.

"There's more in it than I reckoned, seemingly," said he as he turned to Margaret's cell, and opened her wicket to pass in the supper.

"Here's a message for you, Meg, from Master Ewring the miller. Let's see what *you'll* say to it—'Remember!'"

"'Remember!'" cried Margaret in a pained tone. "Don't I always remember? isn't it misery to me to remember? And can't I guess what he means—'Remember from whence thou art fallen, and repent, and do the first works'? Eh, then there's repentance yet for them that have fallen! 'I will fight against thee, *except* thou repent.' God bless you, Bartle: you've given me a buffet and yet a hope."

"That's a proper powerful word, is that!" said Bartle. "Never knew one word do so much afore."

There was more power in that one word from Holy Writ than Bartle guessed. The single word, sent home to their consciences by the Holy Ghost, brought quite different messages to the two to whom it was sent. T♦

John Thurston it did not say, "Remember from whence
hou hast fallen." That was the message with which it
was charged for Margaret. But to John it said, "Call
to remembrance the former days, in which, after that ye
were illuminated, ye endured a great flight of afflictions
. . . knowing in yourselves that ye have in Heaven
a better and an enduring substance. Cast not away
therefore your confidence, which hath great recompense
of reward." That was John's message, and it found
him just on the brink of casting his confidence away, and
stopped him.

Mr. Ewring had never spent an angelet better than
in securing the transmission of that one word, which
was the instrument in God's hand to save two immortal
souls.

As he reached the top of Tenant's Lane, he met
Ursula Felstede, carrying a large bundle, with which
she tried to hide her face, and to slink past. The miller
stopped.

"Good den, Ursula   Wither away?"

"Truly, Master, to the whitster's with this bundle."

The whitster meant what we should now call a dyer
and cleaner.

"Do you mind, Ursula, what the Prophet Daniel
saith, that 'many shall be purified and made white'?
Methinks it is going on now. White, as no fuller on
earth can white them ! May you and I be so cleansed,
friend ! Good den."

Ursula courtesied and escaped, and Mr. Ewring passed
through the gate, and went up to his desolated home.
He stood a moment in the mill door, looking back over
the town which he had just left.

"'The night cometh, when no man can work,'" he
said to himself. "Grant me, Lord, to be about Thy
business until the Master cometh!"

And he knew, while he said it, that in all likelhhood
to him that coming would be in a chariot of fire, and
that to be busied with that work would bring it nearer
and sooner.

CHAPTER XXXVIII.

FILLING THE RANKS.

S Mr. Ewring stood looking out, he saw somebody coming up from the gate towards the mill—a girl, who walked slowly, as if she felt very hot or very tired. The day was warm, but not oppressively so; and he watched her coming languidly up the road, till he saw that it was Amy Clere. What could she want at the mill? Mr. Ewring waited to see.

"Good den, Mistress Amy," said he, as she came nearer.

Amy looked up as if it startled her to be addressed.

"Good den, Master Ewring. Father's sending some corn to be ground, and he desired you to know the last was ground a bit too fine for his liking: would you take the pains to have it coarser ground, an' it please you?"

"I will see to it, Mistress Amy A fine even, methinks?"

"Aye, right fair," replied Amy in that manner which shows that the speaker's thoughts are away elsewhere. But she did not offer to go; she lingered about the mill-door, in the style of one who has something to say which she is puzzled or unwilling to bring out.

"You seem weary," said Mr. Ewring, kindly; "pray you, sit and rest you a space in the porch."

Amy took the seat suggested at once.

"Master Clere is well, I trust?—and Mistress Clere likewise?"

"They are well, I thank you."

Mr. Ewring noticed suddenly that Amy's eyes were full of tears.

"Mistress Amy," said he, "I would not by my good-will be meddlesome in matters that concern me not, but it seemeth me all is scarce well with you. If so be that I can serve you any way, I trust you will say so much."

"Master Ewring, I am the unhappiest maid in all Colchester."

"Truly, I am right sorry to hear it."

"I lack one to help me, and I know not to whom to turn. You could, if——"

"Then in very deed I will. Pray give me to wit how?"

Amy looked up at him. "Master Ewring, I set out for Heaven, and I have lost the way."

"Why, Mistress Amy! surely you know well enough ——"

"No, I don't," she said, cutting him short. "Lack-a-day! I never took no heed when I might have learned it: and now have I no chance to learn, and everything to hinder. I don't know a soul I could ask about it."

"The priest," suggested Mr. Ewring a little con-strainedly. This language astonished him from Nicholas Clere's daughter.

"I don't want the priest's way. He isn't going him-self; or if he is, it's back foremost. Master Ewring, help me! I mean it. I never wist a soul going that way save Bessy Foulkes: and she's got there, and I want to go *her* way. What am I to do?"

Mr. Ewring did not speak for a moment. He was thinking, in the first place, how true it was that "the

blood of the martyrs is the seed of the Church "; and
in the second, what very unlikely subjects God sometimes chooses as the recipients of His grace. One of
the last people in Colchester whom he would have expected to fill Elizabeth Foulkes' vacant place in the ranks
was the girl who sat in the porch, looking up at him with
those anxious, earnest eyes.

"Mistress Amy," he said, "you surely know there is
peril in this path? It were well you should count the
cost afore you enter on it."

"Where is there not peril ?" was the answer. "I
may be slain of lightning to-morrow, or die of some
sudden malady this next month. Can you say surely
that there is more peril of burning than of that? If
not, come to mine help. I must find the way somehow.
Master Ewring, I want to be *safe*! I want to feel that
it will not matter how or when I go, because I know
whither it shall be. And I have lost the way. I
thought I had but to do well and be as good as I could,
and I should sure come out safe. And I have tried that
way awhile, and it serves not. First, I can't be good
when I would : and again, the better I am—as folks
commonly reckon goodness—the worser I feel. There's
somewhat inside me that won't do right; and there's
somewhat else that isn't satisfied when I have done
right ; it wants something more, and I don't know what
it is. Master Ewring, you do. Tell me !"

"Mistress Amy, what think you religion to be ?"

"Nay, I always thought it were being good. If it's
not that, I know not what it is."

"But being good must spring out of something. That
is the flower. What is the seed—that which is to make
you 'be good,' and find it easy and pleasant ?"

"Tell me !" said Amy's eyes more than her words.

"My dear maid, religion is fellowship; living fellow-

ship with the living Lord. It is neither being good nor
doing good, though both will spring out of it. It is an
exchange made between you and the Lord Christ: His
righteousness for your iniquity; His strength for your
weakness; His rich grace for your bankrupt poverty of
all goodness. Mistress Amy, you want Christ our Lord,
and the Holy Ghost, which He shall give you—the new
heart and the right spirit which be His gift, and which
He died to purchase for you."

"That's it!" said Amy, with a light in her eyes.
"But how come you by them?"

"You may have them for the asking—if you do truly
wish it. 'Whosoever *will*, let him take the water of
life.' Know you what St. Austin saith? 'Thou
would'st not now be setting forth to find God, if He
had not first set forth to find thee.' 'For by grace ye
are saved, through faith; and that not of yourselves:
it is the gift of God.' Keep fast hold of that, Mistress
Amy."

"That'll do!" said Amy, under her breath. "I've
got what I want now—if He'll hearken to me. But, O
Master Ewring, I'm not fit to keep fellowship with
Him!"

"Dear maid, you are that which the best and the
worst man in the world are—a sinner that needeth
pardon, a sinner that can be saved only through grace.
Have you the chance to get hold of a Bible, or no?"

"No! Father gave up his to the priest, months
agone. I never cared nought about it while I had it,
and now I've lost the chance."

"Trust the Lord to care for you. He shall send you,
be sure, either the quails or the manna. He'll not let
you starve. He has bound Himself to bring all safe
that trust in Him. And—it looks not like it, verily, yet
it may be that times of liberty shall come again."

"Master Ewring, I've given you a deal of trouble," said Amy, rising suddenly, "and taken ever so much time. But I'm not unthankful, trust me."

"My dear maid, how can Christian men spend time better than in helping a fellow soul on his way towards Heaven? It's not time wasted, be sure."

"No, it's not time wasted!" said Amy, with more feeling than Mr. Ewring had ever seen her show before.

"Farewell, dear maid," said he. "One thing I pray you to remember: what you lack is the Holy Ghost, for He only can show Christ unto you. I or others can talk of Him, but the Spirit alone can reveal Him to your own soul. And the Spirit is promised to them that ask Him."

"I'll not forget, Master. Good even, and God bless you!"

Mr. Ewring stood a moment longer to watch Amy as she ran down the road, with a step tenfold more light and elastic than the weary, languid one with which she had come up.

"God bless the maid!" he said half aloud, "and may He 'stablish, strengthen, settle' her! 'He hath mercy on whom He will have mercy.' But we on whom He has had it aforetime, how unbelieving and hopeless we are apt to be! Verily, the last recruit that I looked to see join Christ's standard was Nicholas Clere's daughter."

CHAPTER XXXIX.

THE LAST MARTYRDOM.

OOD-MORROW, Mistress Clere! Any placards of black velvet have you?"

A placard with us means a large handbill for pasting on walls : in Queen Mary's time they meant by it a double stomacher,—namely an ornamentation for the front of a dress, put on separate from it, which might either be plain silk or velvet, or else worked with beautiful embroidery, gold twist, sometimes even pearls and precious stones."

Mrs. Clere came in all haste and much obsequiousness, for it was no less a person than the Mayoress of Colchester who thus inquired for a black velvet placard."

"We have so, Madam, and right good ones belike. Amy, fetch down yonder box with the bettermost placards."

Amy ran up the little ladder needful to reach the higher shelves, and brought down the box. It was not often that Mrs. Clere was asked for her superior goods, for she dealt chiefly with those whose purses would not stretch so far.

"Here, Madam, is a fine one of carnation velvet— and here a black wrought in gold twist; or what think you of this purple bordered in pearls?"

"That liketh me the best," said the Mayoress

taking up the purple velvet, "What cost it, Mistress Clere?"

"Twenty-six and eightpence, Madam, at your pleasure."

"'Tis dear."

"Nay, Madam! Pray you look on the quality—velvet of the finest, and pearls of right good colour. You shall not find a better in any shop in the town." And Mrs. Clere dexterously turned the purple placard to the light in such a manner that a little spot on one side of it should not show. "Or if this carnation please you the better——"

"No, I pass not upon that," said the Mayoress; which meant, that she did not fancy it. "Will you take four-and-twenty shillings, Mistress Clere?"

It was then considered almost a matter of course that a shopkeeper must be offered less than he asked; and going from shop to shop to "cheapen" the articles they wanted was a common amusement of ladies.

Mrs. Clere looked doubtful. "Well, truly, Madam, I should gain not a penny thereby; yet rather than lose your good custom, seeing for whom it is——"

"Very good," said the Mayoress, put it up."

Amy knew that the purple placard had cost her mother 16s. 8d., and had been slightly damaged since it came into her hands. She knew also that Mrs. Clere would confess the fraud to the priest, would probably be told to repeat the Lord's Prayer three times over as a penance for it, would gabble through the words as fast as possible, and would then consider her sin quite done away with, and her profit of 7s. 4d. cheaply secured. She knew also that the Mayoress, in all probability, was aware that Mrs. Clere's protestation about not gaining a single penny was a mere flourish of words, not at all meant to be accepted as a fact.

"Is there aught of news stirring, an' it like you, Madam?" asked Mrs. Clere, as she rolled up the placard inside out, and secured it with tape.

"I know of none, truly," answered the Mayoress, "save to-morrow's burning, the which I would were over for such spectacles like me not—not that I would save evil folks from the due penalty of their sins, but that I would some less displeasant manner of execution might be found. Truly, what with the heat, and the dust, and the close crowds that gather, 'tis no dainty matter to behold."

"You say truth, Madam. Indeed, the last burning we had, my daughter here was so close pressed in the crowd, and so near the fire, she fair swooned, and had to be borne thence. But who shall suffer to-morrow, an' it like you? for I heard nought thereabout."

Mrs. Clere presented the little parcel as she spoke.

"Only two women," said the Mayoress, taking her purchase: "not nigh so great a burning as the last—so very likely the crowd shall be less also."

The crowd was not much less on the waste place by the Lexden Road, when on the 17th of September, 1557, those two martyrs were brought forth to die: Agnes Bongeor, full of joy and triumph, praising God that at length she was counted worthy to suffer for His Name's sake; Margaret Thurston, the disciple who had denied Him, and for whom therefore there could be no triumph; yet, even now, a meek and fervent appeal from the heart's core, of "Lord, Thou knowest that I love Thee!"

As the chain was being fastened around them a voice came from the crowd—one of those mysterious voices never to be traced to a speaker, perpetually heard at martyrdoms.

"'He remembered that they were but flesh.' 'He

hath remembered His covenant for ever.' 'According to Thy mercy, remember Thou me!'"

Only Margaret Thurston knew who spoke three times that word never to be forgotten, once a terrible rebuke, now and evermore a benediction.

So went home the last of the Colchester martyrs.

As Mr. Ewring turned back, he caught sight of Dorothy Denny, and made his way back to her.

"You come to behold, do you, Dorothy?" said he, when they had turned into a quiet side street, safe from hostile ears.

"Ay, Master, it strengthens me," she said.

"Thou'rt of the right stuff, then," he answered. "It weakens such as be not."

"Eh, I'm as weak as any one," replied Dorothy. "What comforts me is to see how the good Lord can put strength into the very feeblest lamb of all His flock. It seems like as if the Shepherd lifted the lamb into His arms, so that it had no labour to carry itself."

"Ay, 'tis easy to bear a burden, when you and it be borne together," said Mr. Ewring. "Dorothy, have you strength for that burden?"

"Master Ewring, I've given up thinking that I've any strength for any thing, and then I just go and ask for it for everything, and methinks I get along best that way."

"Aye, so? You are coming on fast, Dorothy. Many Christian folks miss that lesson half their lives."

"Well, I don't know but they do the best that are weak," said Dorothy. "Look you, they know it, and know they must fetch better strength than their own : so they don't get thinking they can manage the little things themselves, and only need ask the Lord to see to the great ones."

"It's true, Dorothy. I can't keep from thinking of

poor Jack Thurston; he must be either very hard or very miserable. Let us pray for him, Dorothy. I'm afeared it's a bad sign that he isn't with them this morrow."

"You think he's given in, Master Ewring?"

"I'm doubtful of it, Dorothy."

They walked on for a few minutes without speaking

"I'll try to see Jack again, or pass in a word to him," said Mr. Ewring reflectively.

"Eh, Master Ewring don't you go into peril! The Lord's cause can't afford to lose you. Don't 'ee, now!"

"Dorothy," said Mr. Ewring with a smile, "if the Lord's cause can't afford to lose me, you may be very sure it won't lose me. 'The Lord reigneth, be the people never so impatient.' He is on the throne, not the priests. But in truth, Dorothy, the Lord can afford anything: He is able of these stones to raise up children unto Abraham. 'He Himself knew what He would do,' touching the miracle of the loaves: Andrew didn't know, and Philip hadn't a notion. Let us trust Him, Dorothy, and just go forward and do our duty. We shall not die one moment before the Master calleth us."

CHAPTER XL

GOD SAVE THE QUEEN!

 OME and sit a bit with me, Will. I scarce ever see you now."

Will Johnson, a year older and bigger, scrambled up on the garden seat, and Cissy put her arm round him.

From having been very small of her age, Cissy was suddenly shooting up into a tall, slim, lily-like girl, nearly as white as a lily, and as delicate-looking.

" How are you getting on with the ladies, Will? "

" Oh, middling."

" You know you must learn as much as you can, Will, of aught they teach you that is good. We're being better learned than Father could have learned us, in book-learning and such; and we must mind and pay heed, the rather because maybe we sha'n't have it long."

" I wish you wouldn't talk so about—Father. You're for ever talking about him," said Will uneasily, trying to wriggle himself out of his sister's clasp.

" Not talk about Father ! " exclaimed Cissy indignantly. " Will, whatever do you mean ? I couldn't bear not to talk about Father ! It would seem like as we'd forgotten him. And you must never forget him— never ! "

" I don't like talking about dead folks. And—well,

it's no use hiding it. Look here, Cissy—I'm going to give up."

"Give up what?" Cissy's voice was very low. There might be pain and disappointment in it, but there was no weakness.

"Oh, all this standing out against the nuns. You can go on, if you like being starved and beaten and made to kneel on the chapel floor, and so forth; but I've stood it as long as I can. And—wait a bit, Cis; let me have my say out—I can't see what it signifies, not one bit. What can it matter whether I say my prayers looking at yon image or not? If I said them looking at the moon, or at you, you wouldn't say I was praying to you or the moon. I'm not praying to *it :* only, if they think I am, I sha'n't get thrashed and sent to bed hungred. Don't you see? That can't be idolatry."

Cissy was silent till she had felt her way through the mist ra⸱ed by Will's subterfuge into the clear daylight of truth.

"Shall I tell you what it would be, Will?"

"Well? Some of your queer notions, I reckon."

"Idolatry, with lying and cheating on the top of it. Do you think they make it better?"

"Cis, don't say such ugly words!"

"Isn't it best to call ugly things by their right names?"

"Well, any way, it won't be my fault: it'll be theirs who made me do it."

"Theirs and yours too, Will, if you let them make you."

"I tell you, Cissy, I can't stand it!"

"Father stood more than that," said Cissy in that low, firm voice.

"Oh, don't be always talking about Father! He was a man and could bear things. I've had enough

of it. God Almighty won't be hard on me, if I do
give in."

" Hard, Will ! Do you call it hard when people are
grieved to the heart because you do something which
they'd lay down their lives you shouldn't do? The
Lord did lay down His life for you : and yet you say
that you can't bear a little hunger and a few stripes for
Him ! "

" Cis, you don't know what it is. You're a maid,
and I dare say they don't lay on so hard on you. It's
more than a little, I can tell you."

Cissy knew what it was far better than Will, for he
was a strong boy, on whom hardships fell lightly, while
she had to bear the blows and the hunger with a delicate
and enfeebled frame. But she only said,—

" Will, don't you care for me ? "

" Of course I do, Cis."

" I think the only thing in the world that could break
my heart would be to see you or Nell 'giving in, as you
call it. I couldn't stand that, Will. I can stand anything else. I hoped you cared for God and Father :
but if you won't heed them, I must see if you will listen
to me. It would kill me, Will."

" Oh, come, Cis, don't talk so."

" Won't you go on trying a bit longer, Will ? Any
day the tide may turn. I don't know how, but God
knows. He can bring us out of this prison all in a
minute. You know He keeps count of the hairs on our
heads. Now, Will, you know as well as I do what God
said,—He did not say only, 'Thou shalt not worship
them,' but 'Thou shalt not bow down to them.' Oh
Will, Will! have you forgotten all the texts Father
taught us ?—are you forgetting Father himself ? "

" Cis, I wish you wouldn't ! "

" I wish *you* wouldn't, Will."

"You don't think Father can hear, do you?" asked Will uncomfortably glancing around.

"I hope he can't, indeed, or he'll be sore grieved, even in Heaven, to think what his little Will's coming to."

"Oh, well—come, I'll try a bit longer, Cis, if you—— But I say, I do hope it won't be long, or I *can't* stand it."

That night, or rather in the early hours of the following morning, a horseman came spurring up to the Head Gate of Colchester. He alighted from his panting horse, and threw the reins on its neck.

"Gate, ho!"

Nothing but silence came in answer.

"Gate, ho!" cried the horseman in a louder voice.

"Somebody there?" asked the gatekeeper in a very sleepy voice. "Tarry a minute, will you? I'll be with you anon."

"Tarry!" repeated the horseman with a contemptuous laugh. "Thou'd not want me to tarry if thou knewest what news I bring."

"Good tidings, eh? let's have 'em!" said the gatekeeper in a brisker voice.

"Take them. 'God save the Queen!'"

"Call that tidings? We've sung that this five year."

"Nay you've never sung it yet—not as you will. How if it be 'God save Queen Elizabeth'?"

The gate was dashed open in the unsleepiest way that ever gate was moved.

"You never mean—is the Queen departed?"

"Queen Mary is gone to her reward," replied the horseman gravely. "God save Queen Elizabeth!"

"God be thanked, and praised!"

"Ay, England is free now. A man may speak his

mind, and not die for it.   No more burnings, friend!
no more prison for reading of God's Word! no more
hiding of men's heads in dens and caves of the earth!
God save the Queen! long live the Queen! may the
Queen live for ever!"

It is not often that the old British Lion is so moved
by anything as to roar and dance in his inexpressible
delight.   But now and then he does it; and never did
he dance and roar as he did on that eighteenth of
November, 1558.   All over England, men went wild
with joy.   The terrible weight of the chains in which
she had been held, was never truly felt until they were
thus suddenly knocked from the shackled limbs.   Old,
calm, sober-minded people—nay, grave and stern, pre-
cise and rigid—every manner of man and woman—all
fairly lost their heads, and were like children in their
frantic glee that day   Men who were perfect strangers
were seen in the streets shaking hands with each other
as though they were the dearest friends.   Women who
ordinarily would not of thought of speaking to one
another were kissing each other and calling on each
other to rejoice.   Nobody calmed down until he was so
worn-out that wearied nature absolutely forced him to
repose.   It was seen that day that however she had
been oppressed, compelled to silence, or tortured into
apparent submission, England was Protestant.   The
prophets had prophesied falsely, and the priests borne
rule, but the people had not loved to have it so, as they
very plainly showed.   Colchester had declared for
Mary five years before, because she was the true heir
who had the right to reign, and rebellion was not right
because her religion was wrong: but now that God
delivered them from her awful tyranny, Colchester was
not behind the rest of England in giving thanks to
Him.

We are worse off now. The prophets prophesy falsely, and the priests bear rule by their means. It has not reached to the point it did then; but how soon will it do so?—for, last and worst of all, the people love to have it so. May God awake the people of England! For His mercies' sake, let us not have to say, England flung off the chains of bondage and the sin of idolatry under Queen Elizabeth; but she bound them tight again, of her own will, under Queen Victoria!

CHAPTER XLI.

A BLESSED DAY.

"DOROTHY! Dorothy Denny! Wherever can the woman have got to?"

Mr. Ewring had already tapped several times with his stick on the brick floor of the King's Head kitchen, and had not heard a sound in answer. The clock ticked to and fro, and the tabby cat purred softly as she sat before the fire, and the wood now and then gave a little crackle as it burned gently away, and those were all the signs of life to be seen on the premises.

Getting tired at last, Mr. Ewring went out into the courtyard, and called in his loudest tones—"Do-ro-thy!"

He thought he heard a faint answer of "Coming!" which sounded high up and a long way off: so he went back to the kitchen, and took a seat on the hearth opposite the cat. In a few minutes the sound of running down stairs was audible, and at last Dorothy appeared—her gown pinned up behind, her sleeves rolled up to the elbows, and her entire aspect that of a woman who had just come off hard and dirty work.

"Eh, Master Erwing! but I'm sorry to have kept you a-waiting. Look you, I was mopping out the—— Dear heart, but what is come to you? Has the resurrection happened? for your face looks nigh too glad for aught else."

The gladness died suddenly away, as those words brought to Mr. Ewring the thought of something which could not happen—the memory of the beloved face which for thirty years had been the light of his home, and which he should behold in this world never any more.

"Nay, Dorothy—nay, not that! Yet it will be, one day, thank God! And we have much this morrow to thank God for, whereof I came to tell thee."

"Why, what has come, trow?"

The glad light rose again to Mr. Ewring's eyes.

"Gideon has come, and hath subdued the Midianites!" he answered, with a ring of triumph in his voice. "King David is come, and the Philistines will take flight, and Israel shall sit in peace under his vine and fig-tree. May God save Elizabeth our Queen!"

"Good lack, but you never mean *that*!" cried Dorothy in a voice as delighted as his own. "Why then, Mistress 'll be back to her own, and them poor little dears 'll be delivered from them black snakes, and there 'll be Bible-reading and sermons again."

"Ay, every one of them, I trust. And a man may say what he will that is right, without looking first round to see if a spy be within hearing. We are free, Dorothy, once more."

"Eh, but it do feel like a dream! I shall have to pinch myself to make sure I'm awake. But, Master, do you think it is sure? She haven't changed, think you?"

Mr. Ewring shook his head. "The Lady Elizabeth suffered with us," he said, "and she will not forsake us now. No, Dorothy, she has not changed: she is not one to change. Let us not distrust either her or the Lord. Ah, He knew what He would do! It was to be a sharp, short hour of tribulation, through which

His Church was to pass, to purify, and try, and make her white: and now the land shall have rest forty years, that she may sing to Him a new song on the sea of glass. Those five years have lit the candle of England's Church, and as our good old Bishop said in dying, by God's grace it shall never be put out."

"Well, sure, it's a blessed day!"

"Dorothy, can you compass to drive with me to Hedingham again? I think long till those poor children be rescued. And the nuns will be ready and glad to give them up; they'll not want to be found with Protestant children in their keeping—children, too, of a martyred man."

"Master Ewring, give me but time to get me tidied and my hood, and I'll go with you this minute, if you will. I was mopping out the loft. When Mistress do come back, she shall find her house as clean as she'd have had it if she'd been here, and that's clean enough, I can tell you."

"Right, friend, 'Faithful in a little, faithful also in much.' Dorothy, you'd have made a good martyr."

"Me, Master?"

Mr. Ewring smiled. "Well, whether shall it be to-morrow, or leave over Sunday?"

"If it liked you, Master, I would say to-morrow. Poor little dears! they'll be so pleased to come back to their friends. I can be ready for them—I'll work early and late but I will. Did you think of taking the little lad yourself, or are they all to bide with me?"

"I'll take him the minute he's old enough, and no more needs a woman's hand about him. You know, Dorothy, there be no woman in mine house—now."

"Well, he'll scarce be that yet, I reckon. Howbeit, the first thing is to fetch 'em. Master, when think you Mistress shall be let go?"

"It is hard to say, Dorothy, for we've heard so little. But if she be in the Bishop of London's keeping, as she was, I cast no doubt she shall be delivered early. Doubtless all the bishops that refuse to conform shall be deprived: and he will not conform, without he be a greater rogue than I think."

There was something of the spirit of the earliest Christians when they had all things common, in the matter-of-course way in which it was understood on both sides that each was ready to take charge, at any sacrifice of time, money, or ease, of children who had been left fatherless by martyrdom.

Early the next morning, the miller's cart drew up before the door of the King's Head, and Dorothy, hooded and cloaked, with a round basket on her arm, was quite ready to get in. The drive to Hedingham was pleasant enough, cold as the weather was; and at last they reached the barred gate of the convent. Dorothy alighted from the cart.

"I'll see you let in, Dorothy, ere I leave you," said he, "if indeed I have to leave you at all. I should never marvel if they brought the children forth, and were earnest to be rid of them at once."

It did not seem like it, however, for several knocks were necessary before the wicket unclosed. The portress looked relieved when she saw who was there.

"What would you?" asked she.

Mr. Ewring had given Dorothy advice how to proceed.

"An' it like you, might I see the children? Cicely Johnson and the little ones."

"Come within," said the portress, "and I will inquire."

This appeared more promising. Dorothy was led to the guest-chamber, and was not kept waiting. Only a

few minutes had elapsed when the Prioress herself
appeared.

"You wish to see the children ? " she said.

"I wish to take them with me, if you please,"
answered Dorothy audaciously. "I look for my mistress back shortly, and she was aforetime desirous to
bring them up. I will take the full charge of them,
with your leave."

"Truly, and my leave you shall have. We shall be
right glad to be rid of the charge, for a heavy one it
has been, and a wearisome. A more obstinate, perverse, ungovernable maid than Cicely never came in
my hands."

"Thank the Lord ! " said Dorothy.

"Poor creatures!" said the Prioress. "I suppose
you will do your best to undo our teaching, and their
souls will be lost. Howbeit, we were little like to have
saved them. And it will be well, now for the com-
munity that they should go. Wait, and I will send
them to you."

Dorothy waited half-an-hour. At the end of that
time a door opened in the wainscot, which she had not
known was there, and a tall, pale, slender girl of eleven,
looking older than she was, came forward.

"Dorothy Denny ! " said Cissy's unchanged voice,
in tones of unmistakable delight. "Oh, they didn't tell
me who it was! Are we to go with *you?*—back to
Colchester? Has something happened? Do tell me
what is going to become of us."

"My dear heart, peace and happiness, if it please the
Lord. Master Ewring and I have come to fetch you
all. The Queen is departed to God, and the Lady
Elizabeth is now Queen; and the nuns are ready enough
to be rid of you. If my dear mistress come home safe
—as please God, she shall—you shall be all her chil-

dren, and Master Ewring hath offered to take Will when he be old enough, and learn him his trade. Your troubles be over, I trust the Lord, for some while."

"It's just in time!" said Cissy with a gasp of relief. "Oh, how wicked I have been, not to trust God better! and He was getting this ready for us all the while!"

CHAPTER XLII

WHAT THEY FOUND AT THE KING'S HEAD.

R. EWRING had stayed at the gate, gues-sing that Dorothy would not be long in fulfilling her errand. He cast the reins on the neck of his old bay horse, and al-lowed it to crop the grass while he waited.

Many a short prayer for the success of the journey went up as he sat there. At last the gate was opened, and a boy of seven years old bounded out of it and ran up to the cart.

"Master Ewring, is that you? . I'm glad to see you. We're all coming. Is that old Tim?"

"That's old Tim, be sure," said the miller. "Pat him, Will, and then give me your hand and make a long jump."

Will obeyed, just as the gate opened again, and Dorothy came out of it with the two little girls. Little Nell—no longer Baby—could walk now, and chatter too, though few except Cissy understood what she said. She talked away in a very lively manner, until Dorothy lifted her into the cart, when the sight of Mr. Ewring seemed to exert a paralysing effect upon her, nor was she reassured at once by his smile.

"Dear heart, but it 'll be a close fit!" said Dorothy. "How be we to pack ourselves?"

"Cissy must sit betwixt us," answered the miller;

25'

" she's not quite so fat as a sack of flour. Take the little one on your knees, Dorothy; and Will shall come in front of me, and take his first lesson in driving Tim."

They settled themselves accordingly, Will being highly delighted at his promotion.

" Well, I reckon you are not sorry to be forth of that place? " suggested Mr. Ewring.

" Oh, so glad! " said Cissy, under her breath.

" And how hath Will stood out? " was the next question, which produced profound silence for a few seconds. Then Will broke forth.

" I haven't, Master Ewring—at least, it's Cissy's doing, and she's had hard work to make me stick. I should have given up ever so many times if she'd have let me. I didn't think I could stand it much longer, and it was only last night I told her so, and she begged and prayed me to hold on."

" That's an honest lad," said Mr. Ewring.

" And that's a dear maid," added Dorothy.

" Then Cissy stood out, did she? "

" Cissy! eh, they'd never have got *her* to kneel down to their ugly images, not if they'd cut her head off for it. She's just like a stone wall. Nell did, till Cissy got hold of her and told her not; but she didn't know what it meant, so I hope it wasn't wicked. You see, she's so little, and she forgets what is said to her."

" Ay, ay; poor little dear! " said Dorothy. " And what did they to you, my poor dears, when you wouldn't? "

" Oh, lots of things," said Will. " Beat us sometimes, and shut us in dark cupboards, and sent us to bed without supper. One night they made Cissy—— "

" Never mind, Will," said Cissy blushing.

" But they'd better know," said Will stoutly. " They made Cissy kneel all night on the floor of the dormitory, cied to a bed-post. They said if she wouldn't kneel to the saint, she should kneel without it. And Sister Mary asked her how she liked saying her prayers to the moon."

"Cruel, hard-hearted wretches!" exclaimed Dorothy.

"Then they used to keep us several hours without anything to eat, and at the end of it they would hold out something uncommon good, and just when we were going to take it they'd snatch it away."

"I'll tell you what, if I had known that a bit sooner, they'd have had a piece of my mind," said Dorothy.

"With some thorns on it, I guess," commented the miller.

"Eh, dear, but I marvel if I could have kept my fingers off 'em! And they beat thee, Will?"

"Hard," said Will.

"And thee, Cissy?"

"Yes—sometimes," said Cissy quietly. "But I did not care for that, if they'd have left alone harassing Will. You see, he's younger than me, and he doesn't remember Father as well. If there hadn't been any right and wrong about it, I could not have done what would vex Father."

Tim trotted on for a while, and Will was deeply interested in his driving lesson. About a mile from Colchester, Mr. Ewring rather suddenly pulled up.

"Love! is that you?" he said.

John Love, who was partly hidden by some bushes, came out and showed himself.

"Ay, and I well-nigh marvel it is either you or me," said he significantly.

"Truly, you may say so. I believe we were aforetime the best noted 'heretics' in all Colchester. And yet here we be, on the further side of these five bitter years, left to rejoice together"

"Love, I would your Agnes would look in on me a time or two," said Dorothy. "I have proper little wit touching babes, and she might help me to a thing or twain."

"You'll have as much as the nuns, shouldn't marvel," said Love, smiling. "But I'll bid Agnes look in. You're about to care for the little ones, then?"

"Ay, till they get better care," said Dorothy, simply.

"You'll win the Lord's blessing with them. Good den! By the way, have you heard that Jack Thurston's still staunch?"

"Is he so? I'm right glad."

"Ay, they say—Bartle it was told a neighbour of mine—he's held firm till the priests were fair astonied at him; they thought they'd have brought him round, and that was why they never burned him. He'll come forth now, I guess."

"Not a doubt of it. There shall be some right happy deliverances all over the realm, and many an happy meeting," said Mr. Ewring, with a faint sigh at the thought that no such blessedness was in store for him, until he should reach the gate of the Celestial City. "Good den, Jack."

They drove in at the North Gate, down Balcon Lane, with a passing greeting to Amy Clere, who was taking down mantles at the shop door, and whose whole face lighted up at the sight, and turned through the great archway into the courtyard of the King's Head. The cat came out to meet them, with arched back and erect tail, and began to mew and rub herself against Dorothy, having evidently some deeply interesting communication to make in cat language; but what it was they could not even guess until they reached the kitchen.

"Sure," said Dorothy, "there's somebody here, beside Barbara. Run in, my dears," she added to the children.

"Methinks there must be company in the kitchen, and if Bab be all alone to cook and serve for a dozen, she'll be fain to see me returned. Tell her I'm come, and will be there in a minute, only I'd fain not wake the babe, for she's weary with unwonted sights."

Little Helen had fallen asleep in Dorothy's arms. Cissy and Will went forward into the kitchen. Barbara was there, but instead of company, only one person was seated in the big carved chair before the fire, furnished with red cushions. That was the only sort of easy chair then known.

"Ah, here they are!" said an unexpected voice. "The Lord be praised! I've all my family safe at last."

Dorothy, coming in with little Helen, nearly dropped her in astonished delight.

"Mistress Wade!" cried Mr. Ewring, following her. "Truly, you are a pleasant sight, and I am full fain to welcome you back. I trusted we should so do ere long, but I looked not to behold you thus soon."

"Well, and you are a pleasant sight, Master Ewring, to her eyes that for fourteen months hath seen little beside the sea-coals[1] in the Bishop of London's coalhouse. That's where he sets his prisoners that be principally[2] lodged, and he was pleased to account of me as a great woman," said Mrs. Wade, cheerily. "But we have right good cause to praise God, every one ; and next after that to give some thanks to each other. I've heard much news from Bab, touching many folks and things, and thee not least, Doll. Trust me, I never guessed into how faithful hands all my goods should fall, nor how thou shouldst keep matters going as well as if I had been here mine own self. Thou shalt find

---

[1] Coals: all coal then came to London by sea
[2] Handsomely.

in time to come that I know a true friend and an honest servant, and account of her as much worth. So you are to be my children now and henceforth?—only I hear, Master Ewring, you mean to share the little lad with me. That's right good. What hast thou to say, little Cicely ? "

" Please, Mistress Wade, I think God has taken good care of us, and I only hope He's told Father."

" Dear child, thy father shall lack no telling," said Mr. Ewring. "He is where no shade of mistrust can come betwixt him and God, and he knows with certainty, as the angels do, that all shall be well with you for ever."

Cissy looked up. "Please, may we sing the hymn Rose did, when she was taken down to the dungeon ? "

" Sing, my child, and we will join thee."

" Praise God, from whom all blessings flow,
Praise Him, all creatures here below ;
Praise Him above, ye heavenly host,
Praise Father, Son, and Holy Ghost ! "

" Dear heart ! but that's sweet ! " said Dorothy, wiping her eyes.

" Truth ! but they sing it better *there*," responded Mr Ewring softly.

THE END.

www.ingramcontent.com/pod-product-compliance
Lightning Source LLC
Chambersburg PA
CBHW030800020726
47499CB00006B/1703